Fortress Iron Eyes

Tracking outlaws Dobie Miller and Waldo Schmitt into a deadly desert, the notorious bounty hunter Iron Eyes is closing the distance between them with every beat of his determined heart.

Yet the magnificent palomino stallion beneath his ornate saddle is starting to suffer. For years the deadly Iron Eyes has never been concerned about his horses, but since acquiring the powerful stallion, his attitude has changed.

Iron Eyes knows that the horse has saved his life many times, due to its remarkable strength, but now it needs water badly. Every instinct tells the bounty hunter to stop his relentless hunt for the wanted outlaws, but then his steely eyes spot something out in the sickening heat-haze. It is a towering fortress. Iron Eyes presses on.

Fortress Iron Eyes

Rory Black

A Black Horse Western
ROBERT HALE

© Rory Black 2016
First published in Great Britain 2016
Paperback edition 2018

ISBN 978-0-7198-2833-1

The Crowood Press
The Stable Block
Crowood Lane
Ramsbury
Marlborough
Wiltshire SN8 2HR

www.bhwesterns.com

Robert Hale is an imprint
of The Crowood Press

The right of Rory Black to be identified as
author of this work has been asserted by him
in accordance with the Copyright, Designs and
Patents Act 1988

Typeset by Derek Doyle & Associates, Shaw Heath
Printed and bound in Great Britain by
CPI Group (UK) Ltd, Croydon, CR0 4YY

Dedicated to my beautiful mother Olive.

PROLOGUE

When the civil war eventually ended it became obvious to those who lived and ruled in their marble towers on the eastern seaboard that it was time to open up the vast territories beyond the still smouldering battlefields. With a cunning more natural to foxes than human beings the government decided to encourage its broken people to venture west. They wanted everything beyond the Pecos River settled and soon wagon trains set out to find their own utopia.

The trouble was that the territories were already settled by hundreds of different tribes. Men, women and children travelled aboard their canvas covered prairie schooners into those lands in total ignorance of what they were facing. Soon trouble began to boil over in the cauldron of clashing cultures as more and more white settlers filled the uncharted expanses.

The numerous Indian tribes had always fought amongst themselves and one tribe knew how far they could push another. When the cavalry suddenly arrived and erected forts to guard the wagon trains it soon became obvious that this was a game stacked against the native inhabitants. They became the unwanted guests in what they had always considered to be their own lands. It did not take long before the majority of tribes clashed with the ever growing exodus of uninvited people who filled their territories.

Like all cornered creatures, they fought.

Soon the infamous Indian Wars began.

It was hotter than the very bowels of Hell in the vast rocky canyon as the haggard rider continued to forge on regardless of the potential dangers. The arid terrain reminded the horseman of similar deserts near the Mexican border, yet there was a difference. There were no mountains there, unlike this unholy place.

Towering rocks rose up from the arid sand,

reaching heavenward as though trying to capture the blazing sun and pluck it from the sky.

This was a territory in which even Satan himself would not have chosen to inhabit, but those who did live in this merciless terrain were not here by choice.

They had been transported from their fertile homelands to this devilish place at the points of troopers' rifles. This was worthless land for those whom the government had deemed to be worthless people.

Many had perished during the journey. Even more died after they had reached the valley of stones. Unlike their homeland there was little game for the Indians to hunt here. They had to rely upon a certain ration of steers supplied by the government and administered by agents. Most of the Indian agents were no better than the two wanted outlaws the gaunt bounty hunter had tracked into this place.

Many agents were a lot worse, for they would allow the Indians to starve just so they could profit by the power they held over them.

The hideous bounty hunter did not like this place one bit, for the sandy floor of the desolate valley was as red as blood itself. Green and purple sagebrush seemed to have the hardiness to exist in the valley, alongside a dozen sorts of rattlers and lizards.

Strange insects flew in the air and various types of scorpions roamed freely across the floor of the valley as if oblivious to the scorching heat. The infamous horseman was fearless when it came to creatures that had warm blood flowing in their veins but he had always shied away from tangling with things that crawled on the ground.

That was why he tended to never sleep on the ground when he was hunting his prey. He had always favoured hotel cots, which kept a distance between his scarred flesh and anything that might sting or bite him. The trouble was there seemed to be no sign of anything resembling a bed in this valley of sun-bleached stone. In fact, the skeletal rider had started to wonder if there was anything in this demonic terrain apart from sidewinders and the wanted men he hunted.

Iron Eyes stared through the strands of limp black hair that hung before his mutilated face at the place in to which he had blindly followed Dobie Miller and Waldo Schmitt. He wondered why he had followed them here. Iron Eyes doubted his own sanity in doing so. Over the years he had ridden into many untamed places, but nowhere that resembled this deathly territory.

The horrific figure had heard stories about the scores of tribes who had been evicted from their homelands and remorselessly discarded here. Apparently in the East the ambitious lawmakers saw little difference on the maps of the new land they ruled. It all appeared the same to men with slide-rules. They did not realize or care where they sent the various tribes, as long as it was far away from the fertile soil and the mineral-rich land they craved.

Iron Eyes knew the Sioux had signed peace treaties which were granted in perpetuity; after the true value of the gold-rich Dakotas was discovered the government encouraged prospectors and set-tlers to come into the territory, flanked by cavalry. The Sioux soon learned that perpetuity lasted only seven years in the eyes of the distant Easterners. Other tribes discovered to their cost that it could last an even shorter time.

Whichever tribes had been forcibly brought to the valley of stones, Iron Eyes had a feeling they might not be too happy about it. As sweat trailed down his hideous face he began to wonder who had been dumped here.

11

The air was so hot it burned the bounty hunter's throat as he steered the weary palomino stallion beneath him. This valley was truly an unholy place, Iron Eyes thought. Men would never venture into it unless they were forced to come, or considered it held something valuable that they desired.

Not even the Devil himself would willing choose to stray into this valley of death.

As dust trailed up into the arid air from the hoofs of the muscular stallion its master drew rein and sat motionless upon his ornate Mexican saddle.

Iron Eyes, perched upon the high-shouldered stallion, stared all around him but saw nothing except a thousand ways to die. He had been told that this was a new reservation but there was no sign of anyone. If there were Indians here, they were well hidden.

The notorious bounty hunter steadied his lathered-up mount and told himself that he would soon find the two outlaws he had been trailing for nearly three weeks.

He was closing in on Schmitt and Miller. Soon the unfortunate outlaws would find themselves looking at his Navy Colts.

Then they would die.

Iron Eyes lifted his head and stared with dead

eyes at the land before him. The red sand between the clumps of sagebrush still bore the tracks of the outlaws' horses. Nothing else had passed this way since the two bank robbers had ridden though the valley. The tracks were undisturbed, drawing him deeper into this hellhole.

Time was running out for Miller and Schmitt but the bounty hunter knew that unless he managed to get his hands on his prey pretty soon, his own life would also be hanging by a thread.

The valley between the high rocks and stone walls was no place to dawdle. He had to catch up with them before he and his prized horse were finished off by the desert heat.

Iron Eyes lifted both his arms. Once again his bony fingers forced his matted mane of long black hair off his scarred features as he scanned the horizon for the merest glimpse of his prey.

Few if any bounty hunters would have even considered entering this devilish valley, but Iron Eyes was no ordinary bounty hunter. All he could think about was the price on the heads of the men he chased.

It was the largest bounty he had come across for years.

Far too tempting to simply ignore.

The bounty of $10,000, dead or alive, was a prize that Iron Eyes wanted and intended to get. It was obvious that Schmitt and Miller must have done something really bad to have had such a large bounty placed on their heads.

Iron Eyes shifted on his saddle and looked all around the surrounding rocky walls. He then tilted his head back and briefly stared into the blinding rays of the noon sun.

The cloudless sky only emphasized the blistering heat, but there was nothing Iron Eyes could do about that. He had committed his hide to chasing down both the bank robbers weeks earlier; he knew that he could not quit now.

He had to continue onwards to the bitter resolution.

Iron Eyes exhaled, then reached back for his saddle-bags. His bony digits flipped the leather flap of the closest satchel, found a bottle of whiskey and pulled it towards him.

He pulled its cork with his razor-sharp teeth and then let the fiery liquor burn the sand from his throat. Iron Eyes did not stop swallowing until only half of the glass bottle's contents remained. He pushed the cork back into the neck and then returned the bottle to the leather satchel.

Again the bounty hunter looked into the shimmering haze.

There was no sign of the outlaws – or any other living creature for that matter. He glanced down. The only clue that they had even ridden this way was their horses' hoofmarks in the red sand.

Iron Eyes pulled a cigar from his deep pocket, pushed it between his scarred lips and scratched a match across the silver horn of his saddle.

As the bounty hunter inhaled a distant sound drew his attention. He tossed the match aside and swung his exhausted mount around.

The distant noise sounded like thunder, yet there was not a cloud in the bright blue sky.

'Gunplay,' he muttered.

Smoke trailed between his teeth as he narrowed his eyes and vainly searched the heat haze for the source of the strange sound.

Then he pulled the cigar from his mouth and gathered up his long leathers, preparing to ride, when another, different noise caught his attention.

The bounty hunter leaned back against the cantle of his ornate saddle and shielded his eyes with his left hand.

Then he saw them.

Buzzards circled in the sky. Iron Eyes could see

15

their long necks as the birds stared down at something far below them. The ravenous, wide-winged black birds circled in the cloudless sky silently. As they were passing across the face of the sun Iron Eyes realized why he had not spotted them before.

When carrion-eaters circled the way these birds were doing, it had a name.

It was called the dance of death.

Iron Eyes slapped the stallion's creamy white tail with the ends of his reins and got the animal moving. He stood in his stirrups to take the weight off the horse's back and rode to directly below the buzzards.

Iron Eyes was well aware that buzzards only circled on high thermals of rising air when there was something either dead or dying on the ground. Unlike other creatures, they tended to wait until all of the other animals had eaten their fill and then come to earth. They would consume every last scrap of whatever remained.

As the bounty hunter rode into the suffocatingly hot air he continued to look all around him. Iron Eyes realized that even though he could not see anyone it did not mean that there was not someone out there.

Someone had fired a shot. They might have a

hankering to add another notch to their weapon's grip.

ONE

There were hardly any other shadows as the blinding sun reached its zenith and appeared to remain stationary directly above the intrepid bounty hunter. Iron Eyes remained grim-faced as his bony fingers teased his leathers and guided his exhausted mount to where the buzzard's shadows circled upon the arid sand. Every instinct told the wily hunter to be aware of ambush while, watchfully, he let the palomino find its own pace as they continued towards the buzzards' black shadows.

It seemed to be getting hotter with every passing heartbeat. Clumps of sagebrush were dotted all over the crimson sand like grave-markers for the dead creatures who had fallen victim to the deathly valley.

Then his narrowed bullet-coloured eyes spotted something twenty feet ahead. Whatever it was, it was dead. Iron Eyes eased back on his reins and looped a long thin leg over the neck of his mount. He slid to the ground and sucked the last of the smoke from the remaining few inches of rolled tobacco.

He dropped the cigar butt, then looped the reins around the silver horn of his saddle. The horrific figure strode away from the stallion to the body. Iron Eyes stopped and looked down at the curled-up remains.

The spilled blood had dried upon the blistered flesh. It was impossible to make out who the bounty hunter was looking down upon.

Iron Eyes glanced around the seemingly empty desert and then knelt. He turned the body over on to its back and with his skeletal hand he brushed the sand away from what had once been a face.

It was now unrecognizable.

Death had been slow, he concluded. There was no sign of the rigidity that comes to all dead creatures when they have been dead for a long time. His flared nostrils told him that the body had only just started to decay.

This man had died very slowly. He had been lethally wounded and then left here until every last drop of his blood had drained from his body.

Iron Eyes pulled the clothing from where it clung to the body. He tore the shirt open and stared at the bullet holes. He counted four spread around the chest. Every one was marked by the same dried blood that stained the face.

He wondered who might have done this.

Iron Eyes stood back up. His unblinking gaze darted all around the area. Then he saw what he had been expecting to see. The scarlet sand had been disturbed and, exactly like the hooftracks he had been faithfully following, the marks were pristine.

The bounty hunter stepped over the body and approached the churned-up sand. Years of hunting had honed his expertise in reading the tracks of any living creature.

His stared down at the ground and read the marks as easily as most folks could read a dime novel.

'Two riders came this way and had themselves a fight,' Iron Eyes muttered as he studied the sand between the clumps of sagebrush. 'One rider then took off with both horses.'

Iron Eyes glanced at the body.

No matter how hard he tried to imagine it, he

simply did not recognize in the dead man's face any resemblance to either of the outlaws he was chasing.

'I don't who you are but you ain't Schmitt or Miller,' Iron Eyes said as he started back to his lathered up mount. A hundred questions filled his mind as he paused beside his weary horse.

But Iron Eyes could not answer any of them.

He grabbed his canteen and found that it was empty. The horse needed a drink and, unlike himself, it was not partial to whiskey.

Iron Eyes knew the animal would die if it did not get water into its exhausted body. Unlike all the other horses he had owned over the years, he valued the stallion. He poked a boot into the stirrup and hoisted his aching length back on to the saddle.

He patted the neck of the large horse.

'Reckon I'd better find you some water, boy,' he said. 'If I don't, we'll both be in trouble.'

The gaunt rider jerked the reins to his left and steered the palomino back to where he had last seen the hooftracks of the outlaws' horses.

Iron Eyes had no sooner found the hoof tracks again than his keen eyesight observed something else. He allowed the stallion to meander between the parched sagebrush, then he stopped the weary animal.

'More tracks,' he said through gritted teeth. His eyes burned down at the marks running parallel with the outlaws' trail. He pushed his limp hair off his hideous features and sighed heavily. 'Unshod horsetracks following the same galoots I'm hunting.'

A faint sound like that which he had heard only a few moments earlier caught his attention again. Iron Eyes nodded.

He suddenly knew what the distant sound was.

It was the sound of beating drums and wailing voices echoing off the stony walls of the valley. It was the sound Indians made only when they were in a real bad mood.

Iron Eyes swung the stallion around and spurred.

The dog-tired animal responded to its master's commands and galloped in the same direction as all the hooftracks were headed.

The bounty hunter stood in his stirrups and urged the valiant palomino beneath his Mexican saddle on. The wanted outlaws might not know where they were going but the Indians who were following them surely did.

Out in the shimmering haze there was the one

thing more valuable than gold dust in treacherous territories such as this one. All Iron Eyes had to do was follow the unshod hooftracks and he was confident that they would lead him and his prized palomino to it.

Somewhere ahead there was water.

The Indians would lead him to it and once his canteen was replenished and the stallion's belly was full he would return his attention to Schmitt and Miller and the bounty on their heads. Only one recurring memory troubled the bounty hunter as he cracked his long leathers and headed blindly into the unknown desert.

For some reason every type of Indian that he had ever encountered tended to try and kill him as soon as they set eyes upon his ravaged form. He had never been able to figure out why, but believed it had something to do with the fact that he was known to most tribes as 'the living ghost' or 'he who can never die'.

Some even believed that he was a demon from their ancient legends. A demonic creature sent by an evil spirit to haunt them for all eternity.

Iron Eyes gritted his teeth and snorted. It made no sense but Indians never stopped trying to kill him even though they all appeared to agree that he could not be slain as all other mortal men could be slain. His scarred body bore the evidence of their savage attempts, though.

The grotesque horseman balanced in his stirrups over the floating mane of the faithful animal and thundered into the stifling heat vapour.

Iron Eyes glanced down every few moments at the red sand across which he was travelling. He was still following the tracks left by the Indian's unshod ponies. Still courageously following them to wherever it was that they were leading him.

Even though Iron Eyes hated Indians nearly as much as they hated him, he knew that his horse needed water badly. He was willing to risk their arrows and bullets in order to find the precious liquid.

The sand-coloured stone walls came closer as the valley narrowed. Iron Eyes was well aware that a million pairs of eyes could be watching him and he would not know a thing about it.

Not until bullets or arrows came raining down upon him.

TWO

The arid unholy tract of sun-baked land which had been deemed suitable for a reservation had no trees growing upon it with which to construct the fort that the distant government had ordered to be built in the valley of age-old stone. So the resourceful military had to use what they could in order to obey their masters' command. The fort had to be completed by the time the first Indians were forcibly transported into the harsh, arid valley, in order to keep them under control.

The military resorted to using the same tried and tested methods and materials that the first missionaries had been obliged to use when constructing their religious sanctuaries.

By the time the first tribe had arrived in the valley

the fort was nearly completed. It dominated every-thing within miles and was just large enough to intimidate anyone who cast eyes upon its sturdy walls.

The high-walled fort had been erected using stone and adobe. It cast a mighty shadow, but by the time the last of the unwilling guests had been forcibly brought to the inhospitable valley the fort had been abandoned and its hundreds of troopers transferred to more important military posts.

The Indians who had managed the long trek to the vast desert region were no longer considered a threat to either settlers or soldiers. The valley below the towering rocks was deemed just far enough away from civilization to deter any of the Indians from ever attempting to leave its confines.

The huge fort appeared like a castle from another world as it defied the atrocious elements. Apart from the occasional troop of cavalry and the odd Indian agent, no one ever visited the solid reminder of a distant government's folly. It had been intended to keep the various tribes that had been forcibly transported to this unforgiving terrain under control.

That had been a vain and unrealistic notion.

The numerous tribes which had been brought to

this unholy territory soon began fighting between themselves, trying to establish a natural pecking order similar to that which they had left far behind them in their homelands.

The valley was nothing like the plains that these noble people had once roamed. Caging them in such close confines was a thoughtless act. It was like filling a zoo and forgetting to keep the creatures apart. No amount of scolding will ever stop a puma or a bear from feasting upon its less cunning or powerful neighbours.

Since the departure of the army, the valley had already seen some of the weaker tribes disappear completely. Tribes that had once been hundreds of miles apart were now within swatting distance of one another.

The younger braves were restless and hungry: a dangerous combination at the best of times, and these were far from the best of times.

There was little natural game to be hunted in the parched valley. The Indians knew that even the plentiful animals they had hunted in and around the plains were not to be found in this barren territory.

They were totally reliant upon the rations with which the Indian agent was meant to regularly supply them. This was the only thing that stopped the remaining tribes breaking out from the valley and waging war on those who now occupied their homelands.

But they could not even rely upon that. The unscrupulous agent who had won the government contract to supply the Indians with regular supplies of fresh food soon discovered a more lucrative way of exploiting these pitiful people and earning himself far more than his army contract stipulated. It was something more profitable than illegally selling off most of the allocated steers with which he was meant to supply the Indians for free.

Unknown to the distant government, which had considered the valley amid the rocky cliffs utterly valueless, the agent quickly realized that, in truth, the valley had more gold ore in its rocks than the lands from which the greedy government had evicted the Indians.

Otis Fairchild, the Indian agent, had once been a gold prospector himself and had recognized the precious metal in the shadows of the rocky peaks. Disregarding the consequences of trading whiskey and guns in exchange for wagons of gold ore, the agent decided to go ahead.

What the Indians might do with their newly

acquired weapons once they had consumed the barrels of crude whiskey meant nothing to Fairchild. All the agent wanted was as much ore as they could provide.

Business was business.

He knew that when the various chiefs had enough guns and were well liquored up they might fight amongst themselves before turning their rifle barrels on their true enemies. That would give him enough time to get far away from the desert.

Fairchild was determined that he would leave this place a rich man.

The bloodbath left in his wake would be another excuse for the army to punish the captive natives, the agent reasoned.

On the first day of each month a small wagon train set out from Dry Wells and negotiated a route through the towering rocks towards the abandoned fort. The three sturdy wagons pulled by oxen and mules belonged to Otis Fairchild.

The Indian agent brought his liquor- and rifle-laden covered wagons to the fort to do business once every month, accompanied by five heavily armed hired gunmen. This had already made the agent richer than he had ever imagined possible.

It was also a dangerous trade, to supply aggrieved Indians with whiskey and firearms. A trade that could, at any moment, ignite the powder keg of an even bloodier Indian war than was already raging in the Dakotas.

The trio of covered wagons was approaching the old fort at the same time as several other travellers were converging upon it.

As the lead wagon reached the fortress walls, Otis Fairchild screwed up his rotund features and peered over his team of mules at the dust rising up into the afternoon sky. He turned to his driver and pointed his Winchester.

'You see that, Lane?' he asked Lane Baker.

'Probably just Injuns coming to get their hands on our goods, boss,' the muscular gunman suggested, gripping the long leathers with his rough hands.

Fairchild shook his head in disagreement. 'That's too much dust for it to be Injuns.'

Lane shrugged, then noticed more telltale signs of movement out in the desert. He nudged Fairchild.

'Look over yonder,' he said. 'We got us more visitors coming from there as well.'

Fairchild rubbed his unshaven chin. 'Something

ain't right, Lane. I don't like it.'

'You're dead right, boss.' Baker nodded. He brought the wagon to a halt in the courtyard of the fort and wrapped the reins around the brake pole. 'Seems to me like there's a hell of a lot of folks heading this way.'

'Too many folks for my liking.' Fairchild grabbed a rifle from beneath the wagon seat and cranked its guard. He sat motionless as the two trailing wagons came to a halt beside his own.

The second wagon was manned by Saul Davis and Tom Carter whilst the hired gunmen on the driver's seat of the third were known as Slim Brewster and Pedro Cortez. Each of Fairchild's small gang were crack shots.

'Get down, boys,' Fairchild shouted. He dropped to the sand and raced across the courtyard to the wide-open gates. The agent turned to his men as they descended from the wagons and beckoned them to him. 'Get your rifles and man these walls.'

The five lethal gunmen were paid too well to argue with their paymaster. They grabbed their rifles from the drivers' boxes and rushed across the crimson ground to where Fairchild stood.

Lane Baker was the only one of their number not

to climb the stone steps to the parapet. Baker narrowed his eyes against the blinding sunlight and stared to where Fairchild was looking.

'What you seen, boss?' Baker asked.

Fairchild pointed at three separate plumes of dust that were rising up from different positions and drifting into the cloudless sky. The agent turned to his top gun and frowned.

'It's too darn early for them Injuns to be coming here, Lane,' he informed his top gun. 'Them heathens ain't due here until noon tomorrow. They might be ornery but they're mighty punctual. Who do you figure that is out there, making all that dust?'

Baker was about to answer when he spotted another distant trail of hoof dust rising up into the blue sky from the completely opposite direction. He nudged his employer and pointed.

'Look, boss. There's someone else out yonder,' he observed.

Otis Fairchild rubbed his clenched teeth with a gloved knuckle as his eyes vainly attempted to make out who was kicking up dust.

'Whoever that is, he's coming this way, Lane,' he replied and spat nervously. 'He's making a heap more dust than the others.'

'Sure is,' Baker drawled. 'What'll we do? What if it's the cavalry coming to check on you handing over the steers these Injuns are due, boss? Them soldier boys will be mighty unhappy if they check out your wagons and find them filled with rot-gut whiskey and carbines instead of canned grub.'

'Hush up, Lane,' Fairchild ordered. His mind raced. He knew that Baker was right. If the cavalry were making an unexpected visit to check on him and found he was selling two of the most dangerous and illegal commodities to the Indians they would all be arrested and probably hanged. The hefty agent raised a hand and rested it upon Baker's shoulder.

Lane Baker had never seen Fairchild look so concerned.

'I sure hope you got a plan, boss,' he stated. 'What we're doing is a neck-stretching offence and no mistake.'

Fairchild nodded. 'If that is troopers and they come here we gotta act dumb, Lane. We have to say that we've only just arrived here and found these wagons.'

Baker inhaled and pointed to their horses tied to the tailgates of the wagons. 'It's a good job we brought our saddle mounts with us, boss. Them soldier boys just might believe that story - if that dust is belonging to cavalry.'

The agent's cheek began to twitch nervously.

'If that is soldiers and they don't believe us I want you and the others to kill every one of them, Lane. Savvy?' he said calmly. 'There's one thing about this desert. It's got plenty of sand to bury folks under.'

'Ain't nothing I like better than killing soldier boys wearing blue, boss,' Baker grinned. 'I lost me two brothers to them Union boys in the war.'

Fairchild continued to study the rising dust. It was getting closer with every beat of his heart.

'So much damn dust,' he mumbled anxiously.

Baker placed a boot on the bottom of the stone steps next to the gate. He turned and looked hard at the ruthless Indian agent.

'Who do you figure is heading here, boss?' he asked.

'Whoever it is I got me a feeling we'll find out soon enough, Lane,' Fairchild replied. He started to close the gates and secure them. 'I'm sure glad we'll be on the inside and not out there.'

'If that is strangers how come they all seem to be heading here?' Baker wondered. 'This place ain't exactly on no maps that I've ever heard about.'

Fairchild lowered the crossbar to secure the massive gates and came towards the steps and his henchman.

'This fort is big enough to be seen from nearly every direction, Lane,' he growled. He followed Baker to the high parapet and rested his rifle barrel on the stone wall. 'A blind man could see this damn castle.'

Baker rested a hip on the red sand-coloured stone and cradled his Winchester as though it was a precious child. His gaze darted between the dust clouds. The shimmering heat haze made it impossible to tell how many riders were forging a trail towards the fortress.

'Don't shoot unless the boss tells you to, boys,' Baker yelled at his fellow gunmen. 'We don't wanna make this a bloodbath unless we ain't got no other choice.'

'That's right, boys.' Fairchild agreed with Baker. 'The last thing we need is to start a war we can't win. Who knows how many varmints are headed here? We might be outnumbered.'

Slim Brewster glanced across at Fairchild. 'Least we got plenty of water, boss. We could hold out for weeks with the sweet water that's in that well.'

The agent looked down from their high vantage

point at the well in the courtyard. He nodded in agreement.

'Good thinking, Slim. At least we ain't gonna die of thirst.'

Saul Davis raised his head and gave a grin.

'If the water runs out I'm for drinking the whiskey.' He chuckled.

Pedro Cortez shrugged and shook his head. 'That might be a good way of going blind, *amigo*. If you are afraid of seeing your enemies, that is.'

'How long do you reckon before them *hombres* get here, boss?' Baker asked. He stroked the metal barrel of his repeating rifle.

Fairchild sat on the wall next to his top gun.

'Soon, Lane,' he answered anxiously. His hands gripped his rifle tightly. 'Maybe too soon.'

THREE

The hooftracks continued to lead the intrepid bounty hunter across the stifling expanse of crimson sand into the very heart of the prairie. Spirals of shimmering air rose up like ominous spirits, yet Iron Eyes did not slow his pace; he forged on. His spurs continued to urge the weary palomino into defying its thirst and continue obeying its ghostly master.

The heat was so intense it was like trying to breathe in molten lava, but Iron Eyes refused to allow his own exhaustion to discourage the valiant palomino beneath his Mexican saddle.

For more than ten miles Iron Eyes rode deeper into the sun-baked terrain. Then, as the almost spent mount toiled up a slight rise the bounty hunter's honed instincts suddenly alerted him to the danger that, he sensed, was close.

Faster than the blink of an eye the tall thin horseman dragged his reins up to his chest and stopped his courageous stallion. He leapt from his saddle, then crouched with his reins still gripped in his left hand.

He remained perfectly still amid the small islands of sagebrush growing in the sand. He was like a big cat, allowing the scent of its prey to fill his flared nostrils.

Iron Eyes pulled one of his Navy Colts from his belt and cocked it. Every sinew in his ravaged body told him that there was unseen danger somewhere ahead. It was masked by the shimmering heat haze that surrounded him and his mount, but Iron Eyes knew that it was there, just over the dune.

The bounty hunter gathered his long leathers and swiftly tied them to a clump of sagebrush. He moved forward like a stalking cougar and climbed up the sandy rise until he both saw and heard them.

Iron Eyes lay behind the purple sage and studied the sight that greeted his red-raw eyes.

Five young Indian braves were gathered around a small water hole. They were feverishly filling their large water bags and then draping them over the necks of their painted ponies. The bounty hunter was surprised by the condition of the braves. He had never before seen any Indians look as thin as this quintet of braves.

Iron Eyes narrowed his unblinking eyes and watched them from behind the clump of sage-brush. He had heard that many tribes had been forced from their fertile homelands and brought to this desolate place. The five braves he watched seemed to be Cheyenne, but it was difficult to tell. If they were Cheyenne they were an awful long way from the place he had last encountered them.

The Cheyenne was a people who had been evicted from heaven and discarded in hell, the gruesome bounty hunter thought.

For what seemed like an eternity the bounty hunter watched them until they mounted their bareback ponies and continued following the trail left by the two outlaws.

As they swung their ponies round Iron Eyes saw that one of them had a rifle. The merciless sun danced along its metal barrel. Then, within seconds, the five riders had vanished into the stifling air.

Iron Eyes felt an emotion that was totally alien to his normally cold-hearted nature.

He pitied them.

They were mere shadows of the Cheyenne braves against whom he had battled a few years before. They were not the same as those who had inflicted so much of their venom upon his person. His body was covered in the brutal scars he had received at the hands of the Cheyenne. Yet, scrawny as the five pony riders were, Iron Eyes did not underestimate them. He knew that there were few tribes throughout the vast country that were as deadly as the Cheyenne when riled.

Iron Eyes turned, slid down the sandy slope and then rose to his feet. He released the hammer of his gun before returning it to his belt. His head drooped as he walked back to his waiting mount. The gaunt man paused beside the palomino's shoulder. His mutilated features assumed a troubled expression.

Something was gnawing at his craw.

His bony left hand pulled the leathers free and he led the palomino to the water hole. He knew that all Indians were smart enough to make most of the weapons they needed and knew that the army would never have allowed any of them to keep their rifles.

But one of the quintet of braves had a rifle. It was

not an old one. It was a shining new model.

The skeletal bounty hunter reached the water hole, where the stallion dropped its head and began to drink. Iron Eyes, thoughtful, realized that for any Indian to have a rifle in this unholy terrain meant only one thing.

Someone must have sold it to him.

Then, recalling the dead man he had stumbled upon earlier, he came up with another theory. They might have taken his weapons.

Both possibilities troubled the gaunt figure. Most of the Indians who had lived on the Great Plains were dangerous enough with mere bows and arrows.

Given enough rifles, they might be invincible.

The troubled bounty hunter lifted the satchel flap of his saddle-bag and pulled the last whiskey bottle from it. His icy stare studied its contents. The amber liquor only filled half the bottle. Iron Eyes pulled its cork with his sharp teeth and spat it across the water hole.

His bony hand lifted the bottle neck to his scarred lips. He allowed the whiskey to wash over his tongue and burn a trail down into his innards.

It was like trying to extinguish a fire with kerosene.

As the fumes filled his weary mind, Iron Eyes finished the fiery contents quickly and tossed the empty vessel over his shoulder. He removed his pair of canteens from the saddle horn and unscrewed their stoppers. Holding on to the leather straps he lowered them into the water hole and waited for the canteens to fill with the precious liquid.

The stallion continued to drink as its master tried to think with a sleep-starved mind. The normally confident bounty hunter was dog tired. It was also hard to concentrate when you were being roasted alive, Iron Eyes thought.

His gaze darted to the bubbles that were rising around the canteens. It then returned to the blood-coloured sand and the tracks left by the unshod ponies.

'If them outlaws were'nt so damn valuable I'd try and find me someplace healthier to roam,' he muttered under his breath. 'I sure got me a bad feeling about this hunt.'

When the canteens were full Iron Eyes lifted them from the water hole and screwed their stoppers on tightly. He hung the damp canteens from the silver horn of his saddle, then tapped his long trail coat until he located a few cigars lying amid the bullets in his pockets.

Iron Eyes withdrew one of the cigars, placed it between his teeth and scratched a match with his thumbnail. The flame had barely had time to erupt before he sucked it through the twisted length of the cigar.

The skeletal bounty hunter kept puffing until all that remained of the match was a charred fragment. He tossed it away and filled his lungs with the acrid smoke.

Any normal man would have succumbed to the sleep he craved but the infamous bounty hunter refused ever to admit that he was utterly exhausted. Willpower was the only thing keeping the dishevelled Iron Eyes upright.

Iron Eyes' mind raced.

As smoke filtered through his teeth he resolved to continue on until he had achieved his goal and caught up with Miller and Schmitt.

There was only one course Iron Eyes could ever take and that was to continue trailing the valuable outlaws until the bitter end. Iron Eyes could not do anything except keep tracking his chosen prey. Others might have shied away from the potentially deadly purpose but not Iron Eyes.

He had never feared death for it had been his constant companion throughout his life. It was his theory that the only men who died were those who were afraid of dying. To the lifelong hunter it seemed that it was pointless fearing the inevitable.

Satisfied that its thirst had been thoroughly quenched, the palomino stallion raised its head and shook its long cream-coloured mane. The horse looked at its master as if asking a question that only Iron Eyes could understand.

The bounty hunter gripped his cigar between his teeth and puffed frantically as he stared into the large eyes of his prized mount. He pointed at the stallion as water dripped from the animal's chin.

'Don't look at me like that, horse,' Iron Eyes growled at his mount. 'Your trouble is that you're bloodthirsty. I ain't had me no shuteye since we rode into this desert. I'm too damn tuckered to start killing Injuns just for the fun of it. Besides, they ain't got no bounty on their heads. There just ain't no profit in it. Don't you go worrying none though, I'll do plenty of shooting when we catch up with them outlaws.'

The stallion snorted. Wearily, Iron Eyes patted the animal's neck and poked his boot into the stirrup as his bony fingers gripped the saddle horn. In one fluid action the painfully lean figure lifted his emaciated carcass off the sand and looped his right leg over the high cantle. He steadied himself and stared ahead.

Iron Eyes might have been exhausted but he was still alert enough to realize that where there were five braves there was almost certainly a whole lot more whom he had yet to see.

He chewed on the cigar thoughtfully.

'If there's only five of them Cheyenne trailing Miller and Schmitt I reckon it'll be OK, horse,' Iron Eyes told the stallion as he teased his reins and encouraged the mighty horse to start following the tracks again. 'Mind you, if there happens to be more than five of them feathered varmints, I got me a gut feeling we're in trouble. Mighty big trouble.'

With its master's words still ringing in its ears the newly refreshed animal responded to the urging of the leathers that cracked across its long tail. The palomino lifted its head and started to trot across the blood-coloured ground in pursuit of the fugitives whom Iron Eyes had still not been able to bring to his own brand of justice.

The gaunt bounty hunter rose from his saddle and balanced in his stirrups. He hung over the neck and head of the handsome stallion as it gathered pace.

Smoke trailed from the gruesome face as Iron

45

Eyes bit down upon the twisted length of tobacco and allowed his faithful mount to plough on through the oppressive heat.

As his mane of long dark hair bounced upon his wide shoulders like the wings of a determined eagle closing in on his prey; he was totally unaware of anything. Every cell of his mind could think of only one thing and that was getting both Miller and Schmitt in his gun sights. He dismissed the fact that this was Indian territory and numerous varieties of them had proved to be his most dangerous adversaries over the years. That no longer mattered to him. He had the images of both outlaws etched into his thoughts. Images he had memorized from the two crumpled Wanted posters buried deep in his trail coat pocket beside the handfuls of bullets.

Iron Eyes spat the cigar from his twisted mouth and lashed the mighty palomino with the tails of his long leathers. There was urgency in him now. He sensed that the outlaws were so close he could actually smell their scent.

The sure-footed hoofs of his powerful mount made little or no sound as they churned up the muffling sand and continued into the heart of the vast unnamed desert.

Iron Eyes steered the horse through a maze of sagebrush and then began the long journey down the side of a dune. He could make out the unshod tracks of the Indian ponies to his left, and also the tracks left by the two outlaws.

Then a distant sound alerted the bounty hunter. By the time he had worked out that what he had heard was rifle fire the palomino was halfway down the side of the dune.

He did not hear the second shot.

But he felt its power.

Leaning back to balance his emaciated torso as his horse descended the steep slope of sand Iron Eyes suddenly felt the impact in his guts.

His bony hands released their grip on the reins and went to where the unimaginable pain tormented his belly. Then another bullet carved a route through the shimmering heat haze and glanced across his temple.

The stallion continued down on to the level sand as the brutalized bounty hunter was lifted up like a rag doll and sent flying backwards over his ornate saddle cantle. The stunned bounty hunter spiralled in the hot desert air, leaving a spattering of bloody droplets in his wake.

Before any of the drops of gore could rain down

on to the ground Iron Eyes crashed into the sand heavily. His limp form rolled uncontrollably over and over until it was stopped abruptly by a petrified tree stump.

The unconscious bounty hunter rolled on to his back as blood trailed down his scarred face from the horrific graze.

Within seconds his face was the same hue as the scarlet sand in which it lay.

The stallion trotted back to its fallen master, dropped its head and nudged the motionless figure. Iron Eyes did not respond.

The wide-eyed palomino snorted as the horrific sight of blood flowed from beneath the long black hair of its wounded master and slowly spread across the bounty hunter's already mutilated features.

As if in deadly warning to the unseen rifleman the powerful stallion reared up on to its hind legs and punched at the desert air. Yet no matter how much noise the magnificent palomino created, Iron Eyes still did not move a muscle.

The animal trotted around Iron Eyes, staring down at him, but the wounded bounty hunter was completely oblivious to his mount's actions.

The distressed horse stopped and dragged a hoof across the sand as it guarded the fallen bounty hunter. There was no response.

Iron Eyes just lay in a pool of his own gore.

FOUR

The sound of the echoing shots bounced off the rock-walled valley and greeted both riders as they headed on towards the sun-bleached fortress. The two outlaws had been aiming their exhausted horses towards the strange edifice completely unaware of the fact that the infamous Iron Eyes had been on their trail for days and had been closing the distance between them dramatically since they had entered Indian Territory.

Waldo Schmitt was the first to haul his reins to his chest and stop his mount. With the noise of the shots still ringing in his ears he turned the spent animal as his partner Dobie Miller reined in beside him.

'What in tarnation are you stopping for, Waldo?' Miller asked, rubbing the caked sand from his face. He pointed at the stone edifice. 'We're almost there.'

Schmitt glanced at the distant fortress and then returned his attention to the miles of desert behind them. He held his horse in check as he vainly tried to see beyond the shimmering haze.

'Didn't you hear them shots, Dobie?' he asked, drawing the horse they had taken from the dead man towards him. 'When I hear shots I get a tad curious.'

Miller shrugged. 'Sure I heard them shots, Waldo. I ain't deaf. The thing is whoever was doing that shooting wasn't aiming his hogleg at us so I reckon it ain't none of our business.'

Schmitt dismounted and moved to the spare mount. He lifted the fender and tightened the cinch. He glanced at his partner and then mounted the horse. He pointed to where he thought the sound of firing had come from.

'Somebody back there fired a repeating rifle, Dobie,' he said. He wrapped the reins of his own lathered-up mount around the saddle horn of the fresh one.

As the blistering sun baked his exposed flesh

Miller panted and tried to suck air into his burning lungs.

'So what?' he panted. 'I'm too damn tuckered to fret about gun-happy critters letting off steam, Waldo. All I wanna do is get to where we're going.'

Schmitt teased his horse forward and looked into the eyes of his pal. 'Ain't you the least bit concerned about them rifle shots, Dobie?'

Miller pouted. 'Why should I be? Them shots didn't come in our direction, did they?'

Schmitt continued staring back into the desert.

'That's what I'm talking about, Dobie.' He nodded. 'Somebody fired two shots in the opposite direction to our hides. Don't you find that kinda strange?'

'I guess that is kinda odd,' Miller admitted as he thought about it. 'You reckon some varmint fired at someone else, huh?'

Schmitt nodded. 'Exactly. It means there's someone out there between us and whoever he's using for target practice.'

Miller leaned closer to his pal. His hands toyed with his reins as he asked, 'Who do you figure it is, Waldo?'

'If I knew that, I wouldn't be so worried,' Schmitt answered. 'It might be Injuns. I heard that the army brought a heap of them here to this desert.'

'Why would the army bring Injuns here?'

Schmitt shrugged. 'It's a good way to get rid of your enemies, ain't it?'

'It sure is.' Miller turned his lathered horse around and stared at the distant fort again. The sun was glinting off its stone walls. The outlaw rubbed his jaw. 'You sure were right when you told me about that abandoned old fort, Waldo. It sure looks mighty inviting and no mistake. I'd never have figured there would be anything like that in this god-forsaken place.'

Schmitt swung his fresh mount to face the tempting fort and nodded in agreement.

'And we'll be there in about an hour, Dobie. Then we can drink our fill of the crystal-clear water in its well and tuck in to the canned provisions they stocked it up with. The army sure done us a favour when they built that thing.'

'You reckon it's got beds and the like, Waldo?' Miller asked excitedly.

'It sure has. I seen them.' Schmitt said firmly. 'Hundreds of beds to choose from, Dobie. That place is the best and cheapest hotel between here and Deadwood. The army left everything there when they went north.'

'I sure could use me a nice bed right now.' Miller sighed longingly. 'My bones don't fancy spending another night sleeping out here in the desert.'

Schmitt patted his partner on the back.

'You won't have to sleep under the stars tonight,' he promised. 'We'll be in that fort in about an hour. Then we can rustle up some grub and drink that nice cool water until it pours out of our ears.'

Miller pointed to where the shooting had come from.

'The shooting has stopped, Waldo. Reckon we ain't got nothing to worry about.'

'Damn right.'

Miller grinned. 'How long do you reckon we ought to stay in that fort, Waldo?'

Before Schmitt could answer an arrow came whistling through the dense heat haze towards the outlaws. The deadly projectile came within inches of Miller. The smile vanished from his sun-baked features.

Seconds later more arrows followed the first, each apparently seeking the astonished outlaws. Both Miller and Schmitt were forced to duck in order to avoid being skewered.

The startled outlaws drew their weapons and blasted a deafening volley in reply. No sooner had the red flames left the barrels of their guns than they saw the five young braves emerge from the haze.

Each of them was whooping as they relished the fight which was close at hand. Hanging on to his reins with one hand, Schmitt swung his mount around, holstered his six-shooter and then dragged his Winchester from its leather scabbard.

Defying the venomous arrows cutting through the air to either side of his sweat-soaked body, the outlaw cranked the mechanism over and over again as his index finger squeezed the rifle's trigger. The bullets from the rifle were far more accurate than any of the shots he had discharged from his Colt.

The first two braves were knocked off their bareback ponies and crashed into the unforgiving ground. Schmitt continued to fire his rifle as the remaining three Cheyennes sent arrows flying from their bows.

Schmitt was unafraid. He had roamed around the wilds of the West for years. This was not the first time he had encountered feathered braves hell-bent on his destruction.

He cold-bloodedly pushed the hand-guard down, then pulled it back up and trained his eye along the gleaming barrel as the remaining Indians came closer.

Without a trace of mercy for his targets, Schmitt fired and saw the pitifully thin Indian fall from his charging pony. Before the painted pony had managed to get back on to its unshod hoofs the ruthless outlaw had squeezed off two more shots.

As always his aim was true and deadly.

With gunsmoke trailing from the barrel of his Winchester Schmitt grinned triumphantly at the sight of dead young Cheyennes lying upon the red sand before him.

With painted ponies running aimlessly past him Schmitt calmly sat astride his horse, plucking fresh bullets from his gunbelt and sliding them into the Winchester's magazine.

'I got them, Dobie,' Schmitt boasted as his fingers slid the last bullet into the repeating rifle. He cranked the lever and then rammed the rifle back into its scabbard. 'I killed every damn one of the critters.'

Miller did not respond to his cohort's elation.

Schmitt turned and then knew why.

Dobie Miller was propped against the cantle of his saddle covered in his own gore. He was holding the arrow shaft which had gone through his shoulder. He watched as Schmitt rode up beside him and studied the brutal wound.

'One of them Injuns nearly killed you, Dobie,' Schmitt remarked. He stared at the blood which was streaming from between Miller's fingers as they clutched the shaft of the arrow.

Terrified by his plight, Miller looked up.

'What am I gonna do, Waldo?' he asked fearfully. 'This is bad, ain't it?'

'Don't fret none,' Schmitt told him with a sigh. 'I can fix it.'

'You'd better fix it fast, Waldo,' Miller said. 'I'm bleeding like a stuck pig.'

Schmitt looked up at the fort behind them. 'Reckon we'd best ride as fast as we can for the old fort, Dobie. I can clean that wound up once we get there.'

Miller winced. 'Is it bad, Waldo?'

Schmitt nodded his head.

'Yep, Dobie. It's real bad,' he said honestly.

The outlaws aimed their mounts at the great stone edifice and spurred. A cloud of hoof dust rose up into the cloudless sky above the tortuous desert as the riders whipped their horses on towards the fort at pace.

From the high walls of the fortress six equally ruthless men watched as the two outlaws suddenly came into view and galloped towards the fort.

Lane Baker leaned towards Otis Fairchild and gave a leery smile as he pointed the barrel of his rifle at Schmitt and Miller.

'You want me to kill them *hombres*, boss?' he asked. 'It's an easy shot from up here.'

Fairchild carefully considered the option. It was tempting but he still did not know who was creating the other dust cloud that was approaching the remote fort. He rubbed his neck and stared hard at the approaching riders.

'Leave them riders be, boys,' he said and pointed to the hoof dust rising in the opposite direction. 'We don't wanna go killing anyone before we know who that is out there.'

Baker shook his head sadly. 'Damn it all. I could pluck them varmints clean off their saddles as easy as spit, boss.'

'Me too,' Tom Carter agreed.

'And what would we do if that happens to be the cavalry over yonder, Lane?' Fairchild growled. 'Nope. We gotta be patient, boys.'

Pedro Cortez walked to the very end of the parapet and turned to the five others.

'It's a good job you are cautious, *amigo*,' he said to Fairchild.

Fairchild looked up at the Mexican. 'What you mean, Pedro?'

Cortez rested his rifle on his shoulder and walked back to the rotund businessman. 'I know one of the riders, *amigo*. He is called Waldo Schmitt. He is a very dangerous bandit.'

The others squinted hard into the blinding sunlight at the two horsemen as they closed in on the fortress.

'One of them riders is wounded, boss,' Slim Brewster noted.

'That is not Schmitt,' Cortez said and shrugged.

'Who is this Schmitt critter, Pedro?' Baker queried. 'I ain't ever heard of him.'

'Me neither,' Brewster said. 'Who is he?'

'He is a bandit who can shoot better than any other man I have ever met, *amigo*,' Cortez told them. He placed a cigarette between his lips and struck a match. He exhaled a line of smoke at his boots. 'Do not tangle with him, *amigo*. Schmitt is very dangerous.'

Lane Baker watched as Schmitt and Miller continued on towards the fort at a blistering speed. The closer they got the more evident it was that one of the horsemen was bathed in his own blood.

The hired gun waved his pointing arm at the

riders and then looked Fairchild in the eyes.

'Look. One of them riders looks like he's got an arrow in him, boss.' he said to Fairchild. 'They must have ruffled the feathers of a few Injuns. Them Cheyenne bucks must be mighty upset if they wasted an arrow on that *hombre*.'

'That must be what all the shooting was about, boss,' Saul Davis reasoned. 'If that Schmitt critter is as handy with a gun as Pedro reckons, I figure there's a few dead Injuns lying out in the desert someplace.'

'I sure hope not,' Fairchild said, gulping.

'He must have stopped them Cheyennes permanent, boss,' Baker insisted. 'There ain't any of them following Schmitt and his pard.'

A grim-faced Fairchild stared nervously down at the approaching horsemen, then turned to his men.

'Holy smoke, don't you know what this means? If those two outlaws have been using the Cheyennes for target practice, we're in trouble, boys.' He too gulped.

Baker started back down the stone steps. 'I'll open the gates to let them varmints in, boss.'

Cortez toyed with his rifle and stared at the grim face of Otis Fairchild. It amused the Mexican to see his paymaster drowning in his own sweat. He exhaled a line of smoke at the ground.

'At least we have plenty of liquor, *amigo*.' He smiled pointing at the trio of wagons.

'That whiskey ain't nothing but turpentine with a dash of colour to it, Pedro,' Fairchild said as he focused on the two riders. 'A man could go blind if he drank that stuff. I made it up special for the Injuns, that's all. You don't wanna go blind, do you?'

Cortez flicked the cigarette out into the arid desert and then raised his eyebrows at Fairchild.

'Why not, *amigo?*' He shrugged impishly. 'There is nothing to see here.'

FIVE

Waldo Schmitt led the wounded Dobie Miller through the wide-open gates of the fort and instantly saw the three covered wagons filling the courtyard. Schmitt saw the shadows of the half-dozen men cast on the sand. He hauled rein and drew his .45.

The highly priced outlaw leapt from his mount and aimed his six-shooter at the six men on the high parapet. Using his mount as a shield he remained perfectly motionless as Miller slumped forward, fell from his saddle and crashed on to the ground.

'Who are you?' Schmitt yelled out.

'We are your *amigos*, Waldo,' Cortez replied. He pushed his wide-brimmed sombrero off his face and looked down at the outlaw. 'Do you not remember me?'

Schmitt released the hammer of his weapon.

'Is that you, Pedro?' he called out.

'*Sí, amigo,*' Cortez answered. He made his way down the stone steps to the courtyard. 'Your *amigo* is wounded badly, I think.'

Schmitt looked at the crumpled Miller. 'Reckon he ain't too well, Pedro. He might even be dead.'

The rest of the men followed Cortez across the courtyard to where Miller lay. They stood and watched as both Cortez and Schmitt knelt beside the outlaw.

'Is he dead?' Baker asked.

The outlaw turned his partner over and stared at the gruesome wound. He snapped the arrow and then pulled it out, the pointed tip from the back of Miller's shoulder. Schmitt tossed the blood-sodden wooden remains aside and wiped his gore-covered hand down his shirt front. He glanced across at Cortez as the colourful Mexican pressed his fingers against the side of Miller's neck.

'Is he dead, Pedro?' Schmitt asked.

Cortez could feel the faint pulse.

'His heart is still beating, *amigo,*' he replied.

'Then I better not waste any time tending to my

partner before he joins them Injuns I just killed.'
Schmitt scooped Miller up in his arms and stood
up. The outlaw then made his way to what had once
been the officers' living quarters.

He did not miss a step as he raised his boot and
kicked the door in.

'Boil up some water, Pedro,' he ordered.

Cortez touched the brim of his sombrero. '*Sí,
amigo.*'

Otis Fairchild rubbed his jaw and glanced at the
faces of his men. He was troubled and it showed.

'Get back up on the walls, boys,' he told Davis,
Brewster and Carter. 'Keep watching that hoof dust.
I've got me a feeling that trouble's brewing. Mighty
big trouble.'

Lane Baker bit his lower lip thoughtfully and
stared at the doorway through which Schmitt and
Cortez had disappeared from view.

'I don't know who or what that critter is, boss,' he
stated. 'But whoever he is I reckon he's gonna bring
the law or the Cheyennes down on us.'

Fairchild nodded in agreement. 'You're dead
right, Lane. Did you hear what he just said? He
reckoned he just killed a bunch of Indians, and that
ain't a healthy thing to do in this territory.'

Baker looked at the gates. 'I reckon it might be

wise if we close and bolt the gates again, boss.'

Fairchild looked at Baker. 'Do it and join the boys up on the parapet. I've got me a real bad feeling that the folks we come here to trade with might just try and scalp us.'

Baker nodded and ran to the gates.

SIX

It had been only twenty minutes since Iron Eyes had felt the rifle bullets knock him off his cream-coloured horse. The eyes of the bounty hunter opened wide and stared all around him as he tried to work out where he was and what had happened. He raised his left hand and pressed it against the painful crease on his temple. It had already started to scab in the intense heat of the relentless sun. He tried to move but then felt the pain in his midriff.

The semi-conscious bounty hunter tried to remember what had happened to him. He carefully manipulated his aching body until he was able to view his painful midriff.

After rubbing the sand from his face, Iron Eyes looked at his belly. He began to know why it hurt so badly. The rifle bullet had hit one of the Navy Colts which were tucked into his pants belt. His long fingers carefully pulled both guns from the belt, revealing the severe bruising across his belly. Iron Eyes' bony digits dropped the Navy Colts on the bloody sand beside him.

Slowly he started to recall the few incidents that had resulted in his pitifully lean body ending up on the sand. As his eyes finally cleared he saw that the high-shouldered stallion was staring at him.

'I ain't dead, horse,' Iron Eyes growled. He sat upright and saw the blood streaming through his fingers. 'I'm sure hurting though.'

The bounty hunter rolled on to his knees. He went to rise when he heard the sound of a horse riding towards him. Faster than the blink of an eye the infamous bounty hunter snatched up one of his guns off the sand and cocked its hammer.

He knelt behind the petrified tree stump and listened to the sound of the approaching horse. He could hear the jingling of spurs beyond the sparse brush. He tried to lower his hand from his wound but blood poured from the gash across his temple.

'Damn it all!' Iron Eyes cursed as he was forced to return the palm of his hand to the deep graze. 'I can't see nothing 'cept blood from this eye.'

Iron Eyes rose to his full height and pressed his thin frame against the fossilized tree. He held the gun to his chest and stared through his right eye as the sound grew louder.

Suddenly he saw the horseman.

The rider was holding a primed Winchester in his hands as he controlled the horse with his legs. Iron Eyes squinted at the man atop the tall grey as he stopped his horse.

'Where in tarnation is that skinny varmint?' the horseman asked himself as he cradled the rifle in his hands.

Iron Eyes suddenly remembered where it was that he he had seen the rifle-toting rider before. He had seen the likeness of the man crudely printed on a Wanted poster months previously. Within a heartbeat the notorious bounty hunter recalled the man's name and how much he was worth dead or alive.

'What you doing out here in this desert, Johnny?' Iron Eyes called out.

Johnny Cheeseboro was wanted for murder. The outlaw swung his rifle round and aimed to where he had heard the familiar voice come from.

'Is that you, Iron Eyes?' he asked, trying to get a bead on the painfully thin bounty hunter. 'Why don't you show yourself? Chicken?'

Iron Eyes watched the dark shadow of the horse and rider on the sand as he remained glued to the petrified tree.

'I'm here all right, Johnny,' Iron Eyes called back at the outlaw. 'I didn't figure you for riding through this kind of country.'

'I didn't think you'd be hunting my reward money this far south, Iron Eyes,' Cheeseboro responded. He looped a leg over the neck of his mount and slid to the sand. 'When I spotted you trailing me I figured the only thing to do was kill you.'

'I wasn't following your hide, Johnny,' the bounty hunter shouted back. He kept watching the shadows. 'I'm only here to chase more valuable prey.'

'I'm valuable,' the outlaw snarled as he moved towards the brush. 'I was worth more than two hundred bucks last time I seen a poster.'

Iron Eyes watched as Cheeseboro's shadow moved away from that of his horse.

'You ain't worth as much as Schmitt and Miller, Johnny,' Iron Eyes taunted the outlaw dismissively. 'They're real outlaws, not like you. You just kill like an old woman kills. You're dumb, Johnny. I'm after

Schmitt and Miller cos them boys got class. You ain't worth the cost of bullets.'

Johnny Cheeseboro raced forward with his rifle in his hands, screaming, 'Don't you go belittling me, Iron Eyes. Them critters ain't nothing.'

As the outraged outlaw's shadow told the bounty hunter that he was within ten feet of the tree stump Iron Eyes stepped away from it and squeezed his trigger. A thunderous roar sounded as flame spewed from his gun barrel. The bounty hunter watched as his bullet buckled the outlaw. Cheeseboro fell to his knees and lifted the barrel of his Winchester.

'You bastard!' Cheeseboro snarled, staring at the blood that poured from his body on to the already crimson sand. 'You damn plugged me. I thought you said you wouldn't waste lead on me.'

'I'm a liar, Johnny.' Iron Eyes swiftly cocked and squeezed his trigger again. With another ear-splitting crack a shaft of fiery venom flashed from the Navy Colt.

The bounty hunter watched impassively as Cheeseboro was punched backwards by his second shot. Then he staggered forward and stared down at the lifeless outlaw. He spat.

'That temper of yours will be the death of you,

Johnny,' Iron Eyes said, pushing his smoking Navy Colt back into his belt behind his buckle, next to its twin. 'My error, it already has been.'

SEVEN

The answer to what was making the largest cloud of hoof dust rise up into the sky was soon made evident to the parched men on the high walls of the fort. The surprising truth came thundering out of the shimmering haze on a collision course with the abandoned army stronghold. Their eyes focused on the six exhausted horses as they pulled the stagecoach up the sandy rise. Unsure that the arid desert was not playing tricks on him and the others, Lane Baker cradled the Winchester across his chest and strode to the very edge of the high parapet. He shielded his eyes with a hand from the blinding sun and squinted long and hard.

'It's a stagecoach, boss,' he said in utter bewilderment.

'A what?' Fairchild gasped in surprise. 'Are you sure?'

'Dead sure,' Lane Baker confirmed.

'A stagecoach all the way out here?' Saul Davis questioned. 'That ain't possible, Lane. Your eyes are playing tricks on you.'

Baker shook his head in disbelief. 'I know it's impossible but there it is, Saul. Look at it. A team of six horses headed here with a stagecoach in tow.'

'It's a trick,' Slim Brewster insisted reasonably.

'Who'd use a stagecoach as a trick?' Fairchild retorted. He watched the battered vehicle rock on its springs as it was guided towards the fort. 'Besides, what reason would anyone have to use a stagecoach, of all things, to trick us?'

'We're on official Injun agency business,' Tom Carter added. 'Ain't that right, boss? We're on official business here.'

Fairchild nodded. 'Right, Tom. The trouble is that we ain't exactly got the right cargo in them wagons. But nobody but us knows that.'

Baker narrowed his eyes as they peered through the tormenting heat haze. He rubbed his neck and then glanced at Fairchild and the others.

'Quit fretting, boss,' he said. 'It ain't the law headed this way. That stage has only got one person sitting on the driver's board.'

'Then who do you figure it is, Lane?' Fairchild asked. His eyes refused to focus as well as those of his younger hirelings.

Baker turned to the rest of his cohorts and pointed at the object creating the clouds of hoof dust.

'Do you see what I see, boys?' he asked. He was staring lustfully at the perfectly proportioned female as she swung and cracked a bullwhip above the team of lathered horses.

Davis rubbed his eyes and shook his head. 'I sure hope that ain't a mirage.'

'Me too,' Brewster grunted.

With no clue as to what his men were drooling over, the frustrated Fairchild looked at them in turn before growling at Baker.

'Sure we see it.' he ranted. 'We see the stage-coach thundering towards the fort, Lane. So damn what?'

Baker shook his head and sighed.

'I ain't talking about the stagecoach, boss,' he explained.

'Then what are you piping on about, Lane?' Fairchild pressed.

Lane Baker turned his paymaster round and

pointed outward from their high vantage point to the approaching stagecoach. He whispered in Fairchild's ear:

'Can't you see that sweet little gal, boss?' he asked. 'Can't you see her long golden curls bouncing up and down? Can't you see her tight shirt trying to hold on to them lovely juicy breasts?'

Fairchild squinted into the rising dust and blinding sunlight. 'Oh my sweet mother in heaven. It's a gal driving that stagecoach.'

Baker patted Fairchild on the back. 'A mighty pretty gal by the looks of it, boss.'

'Why is she driving a stagecoach, Lane?' the rotund Fairchild asked. 'And what in tarnation is a young gal doing out in the middle of this god-forsaken place?'

Lane Baker homed his gaze upon the driver and smirked lustfully.

'Who gives a damn, boss?' He chuckled as he rubbed the drool from his mouth. 'There she is and she's heading here. That's all we gotta know. She sure is real healthy-looking though, ain't she?'

Fairchild frowned as he looked into the transfixed face of his top gun. He knew it was pointless trying to reason with Baker when his sap was rising. Baker wanted her and that meant he would probably get her whether she liked it or not.

'She does look mighty buxom now you mention it,' Fairchild agreed nervously.

'And she'll be here darn soon.' Baker sighed heavily and rubbed the palms of his hands together expectantly.

EIGHT

The echoes of the brief but bloody battle between the two ruthless outlaws and the young Cheyenne braves still echoed around the vast desert. Iron Eyes lifted his head and listened to the chilling sounds of death as they slowly ceased. The bounty hunter steered the tall palomino towards the distant fort, from which he knew the deadly encounter had emanated, with even more vengeance burning in his satanic innards.

He swung his head from side to side but could not see the eyes he knew were tracking his every movement. Somewhere out there in the unholy terrain the bounty hunter knew that there were hundreds of Indians. There were possibly other lesser tribes left sharing this god-forsaken land.

Even if they were starved to the brink of extinction, Iron Eyes knew they were far more dangerous than any other breed of man he had ever encountered.

The reason was simple. Indians were like himself and did not fear death. They would fight for what they believed was right no matter what the ultimate cost might be.

Every tribe had its own version of the same saying.

To them, it was always a good day to fight. Always a good time to die.

Iron Eyes lifted his emaciated hand and pushed his long hair off his face. He tightened his eyes and squinted ahead and knew they were right.

It was always a good day to fight. It was an even better day to die. He jabbed his spurs into the flanks of the tall animal and continued to urge it on towards the distant fort and the promise of shelter it offered. He cracked the ends of his long leathers across his mount's cream-coloured tail. The powerful animal did not need much encouragement as it obeyed the grotesque figure upon the ornate saddle.

The palomino had the scent of water filling its flared nostrils as it increased its speed though the sagebrush. Even if the bounty hunter could not sense it, the horse could smell the crystal-clear liquid in the deep well of the abandoned fort.

The sun was starting its gradual descent but it would continue to burn the hide off every living creature below its merciless rays for the next six hours or so.

Only darkness could stop the torture.

Only death could stop the bounty hunter from pursuing his prey. Iron Eyes sat and continued to look directly ahead into the suffocating vapour. The only thing he could see clearly was the massive fort as it towered over the vast arid terrain.

Iron Eyes allowed the stallion to find its own pace as he checked his pair of matched Navy Colts. The rifle bullet which had bounced off one of the guns had done little damage. Satisfied that his weapons were both working perfectly Iron Eyes rammed them back into his pants belt with their grips hanging over the buckle.

Just as his bony hands grabbed hold of his reins again the big stallion abruptly stopped advancing. The palomino came to a stop and its skeletal master was nearly thrown over the animal's noble mane.

Iron Eyes pushed his long black hair off his tortured face and stared down at the bloodstained sand before them. He looped a long leg over the head of the stallion and slid to the ground.

The unholy sight that had stopped his mount in its tracks was sickening even to bounty hunter. He walked away from the stallion and stood amid the slaughter for a few moments.

The sand was littered with the bodies of the five young Cheyenne bucks. It was carnage. Iron Eyes suddenly realized why Schmitt and Miller were so valuable dead or alive and why no lawman had ever managed to get his hands on them.

The scarred bounty hunter walked around the scene of horror for several moments. They had all been killed with devilish accuracy, he told himself.

Even one of their painted ponies had suffered the same fate as its master. Iron Eyes paused and lifted a cigar from his pocket. He rammed it into his mouth and then struck a match as his mind raced.

He filled his lungs with smoke and tossed the spent match aside. He was about to turn back to his horse when his honed instincts alerted him to something.

The churned-up sand led him to where the outlaws had stopped and slain the young braves.

With the long black cigar gripped between his teeth, Iron Eyes strode to the disturbed sand and stared down at it. He knelt and then saw something almost as red as the fine sand itself.

His long fingers touched the sand. His cold-blooded eyes focused upon his fingertips.

'Blood,' he acknowledged.

Iron Eyes rose back to his full height and nodded as his mind thought about the two men he had been hunting for so long.

'One of them outlaws is wounded,' he said as his long thin legs made their way back to the skittish stallion. 'I reckon he's hurt real bad by the amount of blood he's spilled. I sure hope the poor varmint don't die before I get a chance to kill him.'

The grim figure reached the awaiting palomino, grabbed the silver saddle horn and poked his boot into the stirrup. He swung his long leg over the cantle and sat upon the hand-crafted saddle.

Knowing that one of the outlaws he was hunting was pumping blood seemed to reignite his appetite for the chase. It was as though his weary body had been awakened from a deep sleep. Iron Eyes gathered his long leathers up in his painfully thin hands and dragged the palomino hard to his right.

The hideously maimed bounty hunter steered the large horse between the dead obstacles scattered over the hot sand until he reached open ground.

Then he spurred.

NINE

The massive gates were wide open as Squirrel Sally cracked her bullwhip over the traces of her six-horse team and guided the long battle-scarred vehicle through the dry desert air towards the looming fortress. The handsome young female pushed her bare foot down on the brake pole and hauled back on the hefty reins as her stagecoach entered the unexpectedly busy courtyard.

As the team of lathered horses stopped beside the three prairie schooners Sally noticed the half-dozen men who were approaching from all sides.

Sally drew them like flies to ripe fruit.

They were helpless to do anything but obey her unspoken commands. Perhaps it was that strange indefinable fragrance that all females emit to attract unsuspecting menfolk. Maybe it was just the fact that she was a female and they were men starved of everything apart from desire.

Whatever the reason, Sally watched them draw closer.

Yet the feisty female was neither troubled nor disturbed by the sight of so many heavily armed men heading towards her, for she had an innocent belief that no harm ever came to those who lived a pure life. She also had total trust in her prized Winchester and her undoubted ability to use the weapon. Since she had been old enough to load a rifle Sally had been a dead shot.

She calmly sat and stuffed her pipe bowl with tobacco and then chewed upon its stem as her eyes darted from side to side behind her golden mass of curls.

Since she had first ventured away from her ranch with Iron Eyes Sally had been aware that for some reason that she did not quite understand, men tended to look at her in a certain way.

She struck a match, cupped its flame over her pipe bowl and sucked hard. Her eyes darted between the faces of the grinning men as she continued to puff on the stem between her lips. Sally had a vague notion of what they wanted but had no

intention of satisfying them. She tossed the spent
match over her shoulder and shook her head. Her
wavy blond locks fell on to her back as she continued to suck.

Fairchild stood next to her horses.

'Seems to me that you're a little lost, missy,' he
said. 'As far as I know this fort ain't on the stagecoach route.'

Sally spat. 'I own this stagecoach, old-timer. I
ain't shackled by itineraries. I go where I wanna go.'

Baker grinned as he eyed the shapely female.
'You sure are a sight for sore eyes, gal.'

Sally puffed as she watched the men move
around the length of her vehicle and team.

'Nobody told me that this old fort was flush with
menfolk,' she said, brushing the trail dust off her
shirt front provocatively. 'I thought this place was
abandoned.'

'It is normally,' Baker informed the beautiful
female. 'Mr Fairchild here is the Injun agent. We're
here bringing vital supplies.'

Sally removed the pipe from her mouth and
studied the three wagons knowingly.

'What kinda supplies you got in them
schooners?' she asked. 'I'd have thought an agent
would bring cattle to feed the Injuns. Whatever you

85

got under them tarps sure ain't cattle.'

Anxiously Otis Fairchild shouldered his way between his men and stood just below her high perch. The Indian agent could not hide his surprise at the sight of a stagecoach in this treacherous landscape, nor the fact that it was being driven by a young female. But it was her shrewd questions that troubled him the most. He stared up at Sally.

'You ought to shut that pretty mouth of yours, missy,' He said to her. 'It ain't healthy asking too many questions in these parts. Savvy?'

Sally pouted down at the agent. 'That ain't no way to speak to a guest, old-timer.'

'Guest?' Fairchild raised his eyebrows. 'We didn't invite you here, gal. I could have you arrested. This land belongs to the Indians now.'

Sally puffed on her pipe again.

'I'd not get too ornery with me, old-timer.'

'Why the hell not?' Fairchild's face was red as his stubby fingers gripped the side of her battle-scarred stagecoach.

'I might get upset.' Sally put her pipe down and placed her hands in her lap. 'Believe me, you wouldn't like me if I got upset.'

The agent rubbed his face and glared at the female who did not sound as innocent as she looked.

'Who in tarnation are you, girl?' Fairchild managed to ask. 'And what the hell are you doing out here? Don't you know this is a designated Indian reservation? I'm the Injun agent and these are my employees. This is private land.'

Sally fluttered her eyelashes at Fairchild.

'Hell, I ain't figuring on stealing it, old-timer.' Sally grinned. 'Apart from water for me and my team, this silly fort ain't got nothing I want.'

'That ain't the point.' Fairchild was fuming. 'Me and my boys are the only white folks allowed in here. Them Injuns got the right to kill trespassers, you know.'

Sally paused as his words sank into her mind. She looked down at the agent and pointed her pipe stem at him.

'Now you listen up, old-timer. My name's Squirrel Sally,' she revealed forcefully. 'I'm only here cos I'm trying to get ahead of my man. I figured out a short cut across that damn desert would put me ahead of his ornery trail.'

Lane Baker rested a hand on the side of the stagecoach as he leered up at the female.

'You got a man?' He smiled.

Sally nodded firmly. 'I sure have. He's a bounty hunter on the trail of a couple of wanted outlaws he reckons are worth a heap of money. He left me back in Dry Wells when he set out after the varmints. I got bored so I reckoned I'd swing around the tail end of them rocky peaks and get here before him.'

'Tell me about this man of yours,' Baker said, grinning. 'Does he happen to have himself a name?'

'Sounds to me like our sweet little visitor has a dream man.' Carter joked. 'She only sees the critter when she's getting herself some shuteye.'

Squirrel Sally ignored the jibes and looked down at the amused Lane Baker.

'He surely does have himself a name, mister,' she answered. 'He's called Iron Eyes. Have you heard of him?'

Each man's face drained of colour. The gunmen's laughter faded just as speedily as they absorbed the name.

Carter raised an eyebrow. He looked around at the others and backed away from the stagecoach.

'We've heard of him, gal,' he replied.

'The bounty hunter?' Baker asked her.

Sally smiled from her high perch. 'That's him. He's my beloved. My man. He adores me although he don't quite know it yet.'

'Iron Eyes?' Fairchild felt his blood run cold as

he repeated the infamous name. 'He's here in this territory?'

'He's just got to be.' Sally tapped the spent tobacco ash from her pipe bowl, then glanced at the faces of the men who surrounded her. The name of Iron Eyes had disturbed each and every one of them. She wondered why. 'I figured he'd be here by now.'

Fairchild shook his head. 'He ain't here yet, Sally. I reckon he must be lying dead or wounded out in the desert some place. Maybe you ought to water them nags and head on out into the desert to look for him.'

Sally roared with laughter and slapped her thigh.

'Iron Eyes dead?' She repeated the Indian agent's statement. 'There ain't a galoot around that could kill my beloved.'

'There ain't?' Davis asked.

'There sure ain't. Iron Eyes has nine lives. Nobody can get the better of that skinny critter.' Sally looked around the courtyard and then shrugged. 'I reckon he'll be along in a while.'

The thought of the notorious bounty hunter showing up when half of his men were wanted dead or alive worried Fairchild. He cleared his throat and pointed at the gates.

'You can't wait here for him,' Fairchild told her. 'You'd best water and grain your team, gal. Then I think you'd better keep on going.'

Squirrel Sally focused on the wagon and then scratched her neck. 'What you got in them prairie schooners? Must be mighty valuable the way you got that canvas buckled up.'

Each of the men turned towards her. None of them was as fast as the youngster.

Swiftly, Sally grabbed her Winchester off the driver's board beside her and aimed it at them in turn. The startled men all took a step backwards as they watched the female make her way down to the ground.

Sally paused and cranked the rifle's lever. A spent casing few from the Winchester's magazine as a fresh bullet was automatically inserted into the barrel.

'You boys are mighty jittery,' she remarked as she held the rifle trained on them. 'All I did was mention them wagons' cargo and you got all ornery.'

Lane Baker stared at the tiny female. His eyes travelled over her ill-fitting trail gear. She looked as though she had torn everything that could be torn. The knees of her pants were ripped, exposing her knees, and her shirt had either shrunk when washed or had never been quite big enough to cover up her growing breasts. The gunman ran the back of his glove across his mouth.

'You're imagining things, Sally gal,' he said. 'This desert is dangerous enough even without the Injuns.'

'What you got in them schooners?' Sally frowned.

'Legitimate cargo, missy,' Fairchild insisted. 'Why don't you tend to your animals and head on out of here?'

'I'm staying right here until my betrothed arrives, boys,' Sally said calmly, then added, 'I sure hope you ain't got no objections. I'd hate to kill you all.'

Baker took Fairchild to one side and whispered into his boss's ear.

'Them Injuns will be coming here to trade their gold for guns and rot-gut whiskey soon, boss,' he said, looking towards the confident Sally. 'We can't have any outsiders here to witness our business dealings.'

'I know, Lane,' Fairchild agreed. 'It's a hangman's noose for us if the law gets to hear about us trading whiskey and firearms to them Injuns.'

Baker bit his lip. 'What we gonna do?'

91

'That ain't what's bin troubling me the most.' Fairchild rubbed his neck. 'Them Injuns might end up coming here for a different reason, Lane. They might blame us for what happened to their young bucks.'

'Seems to me that we're either gonna get hanged or scalped, boss,' Baker said. He looked at Sally standing beside the stagecoach, holding her Winchester expertly. 'If I'm gonna die then I'm gonna die happy. I'm having me that gal before I get much older.'

Before Fairchild could say another word to his top gun, Cortez moved between them and pointed out beyond the large open gates.

'Look at that, *amigos*,' he said.

Squirrel Sally watched as the men made their way to get a better look at what had caught the attention of the flamboyant Mexican. She blew a lock of golden hair off her beautiful face and followed them to the gate.

'What's got you so all fired up, Pedro?' Fairchild asked as he reached the large open gates. He shielded his eyes from the dazzling sun. 'What you looking at?'

The question did not require answering.

It was obvious.

'Holy smoke.' Fairchild gulped.

'That ain't good.' Brewster sighed heavily.

The diminutive figure of Sally stood ten paces behind the six men as they stared up at the high peaks. From the flat top of a mesa a spiral of smoke rose up into the blue sky. Every so often it puffed in a fashion similar to that which Sally herself had employed when sucking on her corncob pipe.

'War smoke,' she said knowingly.

Otis Fairchild glanced back at the young woman with her trusty Winchester held in her small hands. He strode towards her and looked down into her handsome eyes.

'Are you any good with that rifle, gal?' he barked.

Sally slowly nodded. 'I sure am, old-timer. But why would you need to know that? I thought you was the agent for them Injuns.'

Fairchild shrugged and mopped his sweating brow. 'Listen real hard, missy. I might be the Injun agent but that ain't gonna mean a darn thing to them warriors.'

'Why not?' Sally glared at Fairchild.

'You see, I heard tell that someone has killed a few of their young bucks out in the heart of the desert. Maybe it was your beloved Iron Eyes. Anyway, them Injuns are pretty hard to talk with when they're riled up. Agent or not, they'll kill us all unless we can hold out against them.'

Sally frowned.

'How'd you know that someone killed Injuns out in the desert, mister?' she asked curiously. 'Nobody can see out there from here.'

Fairchild hesitated.

'We all heard the shooting,' Baker offered.

'And we also seen a couple of painted ponies pass here without any Injuns on their backs,' Carter added. 'Stands to reason that someone killed their riders.'

'I'd quit being so nosy if I was you, ma'am,' Baker warned Sally. He studied her disbelieving face as he closed the distance between them.

Sally swung the barrel of her rifle round and aimed it at the gunman's belly. The gesture stopped Baker's advance in its tracks.

'Something don't add up around here,' she said suspiciously.

Fairchild raised a hand to his men.

'Lock these gates up tight, boys,' he ordered. 'I don't like the look of that war smoke.'

His henchmen quickly obeyed his orders.

Sally glanced through her wavy hair at the agent.

'But what happens when my Iron Eyes shows up?'

she asked the agent. 'How in tarnation is he gonna get in here?'

Lane Baker rubbed his jaw and smiled at her. 'Maybe he won't get in here, Sally. Maybe you'll be needing a new man pretty soon.'

She pushed the barrel of her Winchester just below his belt buckle and narrowed her eyes.

'Give me a reason to squeeze this trigger, mister. I'll turn you into a gelding faster than spit.'

Baker backed away from her as the others secured the gates. He was still smiling at the female.

Fairchild exhaled. 'Them gates are the only thing between us and the pearly gates, gal.'

Squirrel Sally shouted: 'You can't leave Iron Eyes out there if them Injuns attack this fort. That would be murder.'

Before Fairchild could respond to the feisty female he saw Waldo Schmitt walk out from the living quarters and stride across the courtyard towards them. Schmitt was covered in the blood of his partner.

Sally stared at the tall outlaw as he advanced.

'I know that *hombre*,' she gasped in surprise.

Fairchild looked at the petite youngster. 'And just how would a little gal like you know that critter?'

Sally curled her finger around the trigger of her repeating rifle.

'I seen his image on one of the Wanted posters Iron Eyes showed me back at Dry Wells,' she whispered. 'He's an outlaw worth a tidy sum.'

Schmitt stopped before Sally and stared at her. A smile crept across his face as she stepped closer to him with her Winchester aimed straight at his belly.

'Hold it right there, fella,' she said coldly.

Schmitt raised his hands. 'Don't shoot, ma'am.'

Fairchild nodded to Baker. The hired gunman lifted his own rifle and brought its metal barrel down forcefully across the back of Sally's head.

Her rifle fell from her hands as she tumbled at the feet of the laughing outlaw. He stepped forward and looked down at the unconscious female.

'Who is she?' Schmitt asked.

'She said her name's Squirrel Sally, Waldo,' Baker answered.

The smile vanished from Schmitt's face. He looked up at Baker and Fairchild.

'Squirrel Sally?' he repeated the name drily. 'Do you know who she belongs to?'

'Iron Eyes,' Baker replied. 'So what?'

Schmitt stepped over the slumbering female and leaned on the secured gates. He looked frightened.

'That means Iron Eyes must be close,' he stated. 'He must be trailing me. That stinking bounty hunter must be near if she's here. I heard stories that she's always dogging Iron Eyes. They call her his shadow.'

Fairchild tilted his head and looked at the devilish outlaw. 'Forget about Iron Eyes, Waldo. How's Miller?'

Schmitt looked at the agent.

'Dead,' he answered. 'Just like I'm gonna be if I don't high-tail it out of here.'

'None of us is going anyplace,' Tom Carter called from the parapet. He pointed to another mesa with smoke rising from its flat top. 'Not if that war smoke is anything to go by.'

They rushed up the stone steps and gathered around Carter as he peered over the sun-bleached wall.

'We're trapped,' Schmitt said anxiously.

Fairchild mopped his brow and thought about the wagons filled with rifles and ammunition.

'At least we got ourselves plenty of ammunition,' he said, glancing down into the courtyard.

'What's the matter, boss?' Brewster asked.

'That female has gone, Slim.' Fairchild pointed down at the sand. 'She was knocked out. How could

97

she be gone?'

Brewster raised an eyebrow. 'Lane ain't nowhere to be seen either, boss.'

TEN

The relentless bounty hunter followed the hoof-tracks through the crimson desert with the dogged determination of a bloodhound on the trail of a racoon. What sparse vegetation there was glistened as the fresh blood caught the rays of the sun. Iron Eyes leaned down from his saddle and ran his hand over the sagebrush. The blood was fresh, his mind told him. He was closing the distance between them with every stride of his high-shouldered palomino.

One of the outlaws was losing not only his blood, he was losing his fight with the Grim Reaper. Iron Eyes wiped his fingers down the side of his stained trail coat and stared into the dazzling sunlight.

Then he diverted his eyes back to the sand and the two sets of hooftracks that had disturbed the otherwise pristine sand.

The outlaws were scared, he thought. Scared of something out here in the blistering desert. They might have figured they were being tracked by the best hunter ever to turn his skills to hunting down wanted souls like themselves, but he doubted it. They might just be trying to reach the dubious sanctuary of the deserted fortress.

Iron Eyes had another theory.

It was one that he did not much care to dwell upon.

His bullet-coloured eyes focused on the sand as the powerful stallion wound its way between clumps of sagebrush and up a steep rise. It palomino snorted loudly as it reached level ground. Iron Eyes raised his scarred face and suddenly saw a sight he had dreaded.

His theory had been right. Iron Eyes felt no satisfaction in being proved correct. Now he felt vulnerable. The brutal slaughter dished out by Miller and Schmitt had caught the attention of the countless other Indians abandoned in the desert.

The skeletal horseman steadied his skittish mount and eased back on its reins until the animal came to a halt beneath him.

The palomino stallion snorted loudly and

dragged at the sand with a hoof as though trying to alert its master to its disapproval.

'Quit bellyaching, horse,' Iron Eyes snarled. He was trying to work out how many of the Indians were already on the desert floor and how close they might be. Most of the Indians he had encountered over the years were never seen unless they wanted to be seen.

Iron Eyes could hear them out beyond the heat haze that continued to rise from the sand. They were there even if he could not see them, he reasoned. They were all around him if his ears were to be trusted.

The Indians were masked from view by the shifting mist that crept out from the sand like the spectres of long-forgotten souls.

The bounty hunter leaned back against his saddle cantle and looked above the haze at the rocky walls of the valley and the high mesas.

Iron Eyes watched the ominous plumes of signal smoke rising from the two mesas and felt his heart quicken. The smoke puffed heavenward as Indians relayed messages across the vast terrain.

Unlike most men of his profession Iron Eyes had learned to read the warning messages hidden in signal smoke long ago. It was an ability which had saved his bacon on more than one occasion.

The bounty hunter knew the gist of what was secreted in the smoke signals. They spoke of finding the five dead braves out in the heart of the desert and of seeing the rider of the large stallion fleeing from the carnage. Iron Eyes knew that the Cheyenne had heard the brutal gun shots but had not seen the outlaws as they rode for the fortress. The warriors had seen him, though, and placed the blame for the barbaric killings on his wide shoulders.

Once again Iron Eyes was caught up in the middle of a mess not of his design or creation.

Trouble was brewing.

'Damn it all!' Iron Eyes cursed as his bony hands gripped his reins tightly. 'Every time I start tracking wanted varmints something else gets in the way.'

The mighty stallion continued to toss its head and strain against its long leathers as the gaunt horseman held it in check and tried to get a bearing on where the unseen Indians actually were. His well-seasoned instincts sensed they were not only on both sides of him but behind him too.

'I hate Injuns,' Iron Eyes rasped. 'I hate Injuns almost as bad as they hates me.'

His limp hair hung over his horrifically scarred

features as the weary horseman lifted one of his canteens and poured the contents over the stallion's in an attempt to refresh the animal. When the canteen was empty he screwed the stopper back on and hung it from the silver saddle horn.

'That ought to wake you up, horse,' he snarled.

The route that led to the fort seemed the only unobstructed course available to the emaciated bounty hunter. Iron Eyes looked up at the massive stone edifice a couple of miles ahead of him and sighed heavily. He tried to think of what had got his sorry hide in this trouble but nothing came to mind. All he had done was trail two wanted outlaws: now he feared that he was surrounded.

The fort looked like nothing he had ever seen before.

Iron Eyes had heard tales of sturdy stone castles in far-off countries. In his tired mind he considered the abandoned fort to be just like them.

The hooftracks indicated that the outlaws must have headed there as well. Soon the hunter and the hunted would meet, the bounty hunter reasoned.

A cruel smirk carved its way across his mutilated face as the notion of the forthcoming fight filled his thoughts. Soon he would catch up with them. Soon he would kill them or die trying.

Ignoring the fact that the arid desert was becoming even more deadly with each passing beat of his pounding heart Iron Eyes slid his long thin fingers into his coat pocket and pulled a twisted black cigar from its depths.

With the thought of the wanted outlaws burning into his mind, he placed the long tobacco stick between his teeth and then found a match. His thumbnail scratched the match. It erupted into flame as his unblinking eyes continued to search for any sign of the warriors he knew were closing in on his fearless form.

He inhaled the acrid smoke and tossed the spent match at the sand. As he inhaled deeply his mind tried to think, but there seemed to be only one option open to him.

Iron Eyes realized that he had to continue on his present course.

There was no other option.

He looked at the fort. Its impressive walls rose above the shimmering heat haze and almost seemed to touch the sky. He continued to enjoy his smoke, allowing the stallion to rest.

When he set off again for the fort Iron Eyes knew that he might be headed into the gun sights of the outlaw's weaponry, but to remain in the merciless desert was just as deadly.

The exhausted bounty hunter tapped his spurs to set the palomino walking towards the distant fortress. He sucked every last gasp of the acrid smoke from his cigar before tossing it aside.

His long thin fingers gathered the leathers in their bony grip. He rose in his stirrups and balanced on the shoulders of the mighty stallion. The fearsome figure cracked his reins across the cream-coloured tail of the palomino.

The horse responded, increasing its pace. The weary bounty hunter looked to his side and then saw the ominous sight he had expected.

A line of Cheyenne riders broke through the haze and paused on a ridge, the sunlight glancing menacingly off their shields.

With his mane of long hair beating on his wide shoulders like the wings of a ravenous vulture Iron Eyes lashed his long leathers across the shoulders of his mount until the palomino gained pace.

Iron Eyes knew that he had to reach the fortress before the Cheyennes reached him. As the stallion broke into a gallop its master glanced at the twenty braves as they sat astride their motionless ponies.

They watched but did not move.

Then suddenly another line of emaciated warriors appeared from the heat haze to his left. They too held their painted ponies in check and watched the pitifully thin rider as he rode between their ranks. Iron Eyes lowered his thin frame down on to his saddle and drove his spurs into the golden flesh of the galloping animal.

The palomino bolted.

Even though they appeared more dead than alive the Cheyennes were still an awful sight to an exhausted bounty hunter in desperate need of sleep.

His stallion continued to gallop away from the two lines of feathered horsemen. Iron Eyes was well aware that if they unleashed their arrows from both sides his dogged hunt for the valuable outlaws was over.

Not even he could survive being caught in their crossfire.

For what seemed the longest time both lines of watchful warriors did not move. They simply remained astride their small painted ponies and observed the scarecrow of a man trying to urge his highly decorated mount to flee.

Then, like released coiled springs, every single one of the Cheyennes sprang into action. Their ponies leapt from the sandy rise and started to gallop after the muscular mount beneath the saddle of the notorious Iron Eyes. Sand was kicked up from the unshod hoofs of the Indian horses as they pounded across the ground after the emaciated bounty hunter atop the far larger stallion.

Chilling yelps sounded across the arid terrain as the Cheyenne hounds spread out after the fleeing fox. They charged after their prey and set arrows to bows.

As the palomino stallion stretched out its long legs and ate up the blistering sand Iron Eyes swung around on his saddle and glanced behind him. He turned back and spurred the high-shouldered horse towards the fortress. A fortress he could barely see as the sun dazzled and tortured his narrowed eyes.

Iron Eyes frantically lashed his reins to either side of the horse as he heard the Indians release their arrows from their bows. Even though his mount was at full gallop Iron Eyes hauled his reins hard to his left in an attempt to avoid being skewered by the lethal shafts.

The arrows rained down upon him. It was like listening to a swarm of giant hornets coming after him. The air crackled as if a buzz-saw was after his hide.

107

Iron Eyes knew that any one of the arrows could kill him or his horse should it find its target. It was a thought that encouraged the weary horseman to keep forcing his mount on to a pace it would seem to be no longer capable of.

More arrows came flying from the clouds of hoof-raised dust and carved paths through the air to either side of the fearless rider as well as passing over his rocking body as it clung to the Mexican saddle.

Iron Eyes knew that normally his well-built mount was more than a match for the scrawny ponies behind him. Yet they were fresh and his tall stallion had not slept or rested for any longer than its weary master.

The grimacing bounty hunter wondered whether in its present condition the palomino could beat the Cheyenne ponies to the sanctuary of the fort.

He mercilessly whipped the animal's shoulders with the tails of his long leathers, steering to his left and right as more lethal missiles came whistling through the air.

The arrows became embedded into the sand and sagebrush as Iron Eyes kicked his spurs back and forced the stallion to leap over them.

This ain't good, he thought.

Iron Eyes glanced back and then concentrated

on what still lay ahead of him. Every sinew in his battle-scarred body knew that the half-starved Cheyennes were getting closer.

The bounty hunter forced his mount up a scarlet slope and listened to the spine-chilling calls of his pursuers. An arrow tore through the air and ripped through the tails of his trail coat. It took every scrap of the bounty hunter's dwindling strength to stop himself being dragged from the saddle by the projectile's force.

Then another arrow glanced off his shoulder. Its honed tip grazed his painfully lean arm.

Iron Eyes hung on to the silver horn of his saddle and yelled out to the flagging palomino. The horse heard the cries of its master and somehow responded again.

The stallion was now thundering at a pace that the gaunt rider knew it could never maintain, yet he had to try and escape the retribution he knew the Cheyennes were determined to dish out.

The exhausted horseman dragged one of his Navy Colts from his belt. His thumb cocked the weapon's hammer as he turned to face his pursuers as they emerged from the hoof-raised dust.

Iron Eyes hung over the neck of the still galloping stallion, trying to avoid another deadly barrage of arrows as they cut through the air.

The whooping of the Cheyennes grew louder and louder as the small ponies gained on the fleeing bounty hunter. Iron Eyes felt the stallion stagger as an arrow embedded itself into the high saddle cantle behind his skinny back.

Iron Eyes raised his pathetically thin arm and fired at the warriors in a desperate attempt to fend them off. As his bullets tore through the choking dust he saw one of them plucked off his pony. Iron Eyes cocked the six-shooter again as the stallion kept on galloping towards the fort. He blasted the Navy Colt but they kept on coming with only one thought in their minds.

They wanted revenge for their dead, and they believed that the man they were chasing was responsible. Only one thing could quench their thirst for his death and that was killing the ghost-like creature who had invaded their desolate land.

The Cheyennes unleashed more arrows. Each one chased the monstrous apparition as his blood-stained coat tails beat the air like a war-torn military standard.

This time the arrows got even closer to his miserable hide. So close that they nearly dragged him from his saddle. The bounty hunter felt at least two arrows tear through the flapping fabric of his long coat. Somehow Iron Eyes managed to remain astride his faithful horse.

Recovering his balance, Iron Eyes stretched his thin arm out behind him and fired over and over again. Like so many previous battles this was a fight not of his making. Yet just like all of the other deadly encounters, he would not shy away from killing anyone who tried to kill him.

The stallion was now less than 200 yards from the fortress. Iron Eyes abruptly dragged on his reins and turned the palomino closer to the nearest of its stone walls. He then spurred the valiant horse and drove on towards the gates.

The large animal did not miss a stride. It snorted as it fought against its bit in its attempt to reach the gates.

As Iron Eyes squinted over the top of his mount's mane he saw a sight that chilled him to his very marrow. The gates appeared to be locked up tight.

His mind raced as a million questions tore through it. Could the gates be locked?

Then he recalled the pair of outlaws who had obviously reached this place before him. He screamed out in manic fury as his mount drew closer to the grey edifice. He stared at the sturdy wooden gates in the same way as he stared at wanted outlaws just before he dished out his own brand of permanent justice.

Every tormented sinew in his brutalized body hated the locked portals more than he had ever hated anything before. They were stopping him from finding a few fleeting moments of safety.

With a strength he thought had long deserted him, Iron Eyes hauled his reins to his chest and stopped the palomino in its tracks.

The large horse halted close to the big gates.

Iron Eyes' fists pounded feverishly on the unmoving gates. He only stopped when a dozen or more Cheyenne arrows embedded themslves into the wood just above his head.

Iron Eyes swung on his saddle and stared at the Indian braves as they drew closer to him. His eyes burned through the hanging dust at them. Then he saw something suddenly emerge from its depths.

It was another arrow and it was heading straight at him.

The bounty hunter was trying to move when he felt it hit his side hard. Torturous pain instantly ripped through his weary frame, just as the arrow had done. Iron Eyes twisted on his saddle and felt himself falling to the ground.

Iron Eyes hit the ground hard.

ELEVEN

Even though Iron Eyes was dazed, the sound of the whooping Cheyenne warriors quickly brought him back to his senses. The gaunt bounty hunter scrambled to his feet and staggered to his mount. Iron Eyes stared at the approaching Indians and pulled his coiled rope free of the saddle horn. He ran the few yards to the closed gates and looked up at the fort's parapet. He swung the rope above his head as arrows rained all around him, then he released the wide lasso. As the wooden gates were peppered with even more lethal arrows his narrowed eyes watched as the rope loop went upward and encircled one of the blocks of the crenellated parapet.

As the large rope loop encompassed a block of carved stone Iron Eyes pulled on its length and tightened the lasso until it was taut. He stepped into his stirrup and climbed on top of the saddle. Then, with the rope wrapped around his thin body, Iron Eyes hauled his wounded form up the fortress wall.

Arrows flew and became embedded in the wooden gates as the gruesome bounty hunter scrambled up towards the parapet. He moved at a speed that only a lean man could have managed.

His mule-ear boots scraped across the rough surface of the wall as he pulled his wounded body towards the edge of the battlements.

Seconds later Iron Eyes reached the top of the wall and threw himself on to the parapet. He then pulled the saddle rope up after him and dropped it at his feet. Suddenly half a dozen deadly arrows cut through the dusty desert air and shattered into a hundred fragments as they collided with the solid stone blocks.

The emaciated bounty hunter was showered in debris. Iron Eyes brushed the fragments from him and ran to the end of the long parapet. He leaned over it and cocked one of his Navy Colts. Iron Eyes fired down at his palomino stallion in an attempt to get his prized horse away from the danger which was in hot pursuit. The bullet hit the sand just behind the hind legs of the animal and kicked up dust. The powerful animal trotted away from the fort.

Within seconds the Cheyennes galloped up to the gates and gathered below the bounty hunter's vantage point. They started pounding upon the wooden gates and unleashing arrows at the man they sought to kill.

Iron Eyes ducked and backed away from the parapet as a flurry of arrows flew up from the Indians' bows. He had only just steadied himself when he felt a jagged pain in his side.

He looked down at his bloody torn shirt.

The bounty hunter saw the deep gash in his side. Iron Eyes rammed his six-shooter into his coat pocket and peeled his blood-soaked shirt away from the severe wound.

'So that's what knocked me off my horse,' he growled angrily.

An arrow had carved a deep groove out of his already scarred flesh. Iron Eyes looked at the ribs it had exposed as blood flowed from the brutal wound.

Iron Eyes held his bony fingers against the gash and turned. He was about to make his way down into the courtyard when he saw the sun dancing on the rifle barrels that were now pointing at his bleeding body.

His bullet-coloured eyes stared at the men who stood before him on the high battlements above the courtyard. Iron Eyes was surprised by the sight of so many men when he had expected to find only two outlaws within the fort.

'So you're the famed Iron Eyes?' Fairchild said as his men kept their weaponry trained on the wounded bounty hunter.

'How'd you know my name?' Iron Eyes asked. Blood was trickling from between his fingers as they vainly tried to stem the crimson flow.

Knowing grins appeared on the lips of the men facing him.

'We were expecting you,' Brewster said.

'We had us a visitor here who spilled the beans about you, Iron Eyes,' Carter added.

The bounty hunter lowered his head until his mane of long black hair fell in front of his hideous features. His eyes stared downward through the limp strands and he saw the familiar battle-weary stagecoach standing beside the three covered wagons. There was only one stagecoach as beat up as that one, he thought. Squirrel Sally must be close.

Defiantly Iron Eyes shuffled towards the guns.

'You better not have hurt her,' he warned.

Waldo Schmitt stepped forward and cocked the hammer of his .45. He held it out at arm's length and rammed its barrel against Iron Eyes' head.

'She told us that you were hunting me and my pard, Iron Eyes,' he snarled. 'Give me a reason why I shouldn't kill your rotten hide.'

Iron Eyes glanced at their faces. 'Where is your pard, Schmitt? Where's Miller?'

'Dead,' Schmitt answered. 'One of them Injuns killed him with an arrow.'

'Ain't that a crying shame.' Iron Eyes smiled, then repeated: 'Where's Squirrel Sally?'

Schmitt did not answer the question. Instead he looked at the men who flanked his shoulders and started to rant triumphantly, jabbing the barrel of his gun repeatedly at Iron Eyes' scarred brow.

'So this is the bounty hunter we've heard all them tall stories about, boys,' he mocked. 'He don't look as dangerous as them tall tales say he is, does he? In fact he looks plumb pitiful if you ask me.'

Iron Eyes glared at the outlaw. 'You'd better not have hurt my Squirrel Sally, Schmitt.'

'Why not?' Schmitt asked.

'This pitiful bounty hunter might rip your heart out if you've harmed a hair on that gal's head,' Iron

Eyes whispered. His cold eyes burned into the wanted man. 'That's why.'

The smile faded from Schmitt's face.

Fairchild snapped his fingers. 'Get his guns.'

Saul Davis moved to the the tall bounty hunter's side and dragged one of the Navy Colts from the trail coat pocket. He tossed it down into the courtyard, then pulled its equally lethal twin from Iron Eyes' belt.

Iron Eyes neither moved a muscle nor blinked. He simply concentrated on the outlaw before him and thought about the Wanted poster buried deep in his pocket with Schmitt's likeness upon it.

'I reckoned Iron Eyes would be a whole lot healthier looking, boys,' Davis joked as he threw the second gun down on to the sand below the parapet. 'Hell, he looks real feeble to me.'

'He sure does,' Schmitt agreed. His clenched fist smashed into the bounty hunter's jaw. The sound of teeth splintering filled the desert air.

Stunned, Iron Eyes dropped on to one knee and spat blood at his boot. He said nothing as he remained crouched below the parapet.

'We ought to toss his worthless hide to the Cheyennes,' Schmitt suggested, looking down on the kneeling bounty hunter. 'They seem to have blamed him for what me and Dobie done to their young bucks. Stands to reason that having his scrawny carcass might just satisfy them.'

'That makes sense, boss,' Brewster said to Fairchild.

'Then we can trade the whiskey and guns to them, boss,' Davis added.

Schmitt grinned and rubbed his unshaven jaw. 'So that's what you've got hidden under that canvas.'

Fairchild nodded to Schmitt. 'I'm willing to share if we can get them Cheyennes calmed down. Throwing Iron Eyes to them sounds like a real smart notion, Waldo.'

The Indian agent stepped closer to the kneeling bounty hunter and kicked him hard. He shouted into his ear.

'Ain't you gonna say something, Iron Eyes?' Fairchild demanded. 'Maybe you like the idea of being sacrificed to our red brothers. Do you, huh? Do you have a hankering to get your stinking hide skinned by a bunch of ornery Cheyennes?'

Silently Iron Eyes raised his head. He shook his mane of long black hair off his brutalized face and glared at his questioners with dead eyes.

Each of the rifle-toting men shied fearfully away

from his horrifically scarred face as blood ran from his mouth and dripped from the gash in his side. None of them had actually believed the stories about his mutilated features until now that they were seeing them. It seemed impossible to the gunmen that anyone could bear the scars of his every battle on his face. Each of them had heard of Iron Eyes but none of them had ever considered the stories to be true.

They believed their own eyes now though.

'He ain't human,' the shocked Brewster gasped. 'Look at that face. No man ever looked like that.'

'No living man, anyways.' Schmitt swallowed hard.

The bounty hunter lowered his head again. His long mane covered his hideous face from the nervous eyes of the six men who surrounded him. This was no living person who knelt before them on the high battlements as arrows still flew over the fortress walls. This was something else, something far more frightening.

This was a monster masquerading as a man. An aberration created in their most terrifying nightmares.

This was Iron Eyes.

Although they had been petrified by the sight of

his maimed face the gunmen wrongly believed that the unarmed bounty hunter was at their mercy. They thought that their weaponry impressed him and had frightened him into submission. But Iron Eyes had never feared death, and that was the worst any of them could do to him.

As the sun beat down upon them they made the mistake so many others had made over the years when faced with the infamous bounty hunter. They underestimated him. They forgot the one vital thing that none of them should ever have forgotten. Whatever this kneeling man was or wherever he had been created, he was still uncommonly dangerous.

This was no ordinary unarmed bounty hunter silently kneeling before them.

This was Iron Eyes.

TWELVE

Inside the living quarters of the fort Squirrel Sally started to regain consciousness as Lane Baker dragged her by her small bare ankles towards one of its many rooms. The hired gunman was looking for a cot upon which to ravage the youngster. Sally was still stunned by the rifle blow which had knocked her senseless, but as her eyes cleared she began to realize what was happening to her.

She was face down and being hauled across a flagstone floor; she did not care for the indignity. As Baker continued to drag her along the ground down one of the fort's many corridors Sally realized that her shirt was torn to shreds beneath her. The feisty female started to wriggle but Lane Baker continued to drag his prize catch towards one of the rooms. He glanced inside it and saw what he had been looking for.

The cot was standard army issue, complete with a two-inch-thick mattress.

'This is it.' Baker chuckled.

'Let me go, you dirty sidewinder,' Sally protested at the top of her lungs. Vainly she attempted to dig her fingernails into the stone flooring. 'I'll surely kill you if you don't.'

Nothing she could say had any chance of stopping Baker doing what he had been planning since first setting eyes upon Sally. Baker was ruled by his lusty appetite now. His sap had risen and there was only one cure for that affliction.

'You ain't gonna kill me, gal,' Baker said, dragging her helpless petite body into the room. He released his grip and closed the door. 'You're gonna pleasure me instead. From now on I'm your man. You belong to me.'

'Pleasure you?' Sally spat the dust from her mouth and pushed herself up on to her hands and knees. She looked down at her shirt as it hung to either side of her breasts. Its frail fabric had been ripped away from her young flesh. She grabbed both sides of her shirt and then rolled over so that she was seated. She frowned and looked up at the hired gunman, who was triumphantly smiling down at her. 'What in tarnation are you grinning at, mister?'

'I'm grinning at you, little missy,' Baker answered. He pointed at her barely concealed breasts and then rubbed his aching groin. 'Admit it. You might as well give up and let me have some fun.'

Squirrel Sally snorted angrily. Carefully she got back to her feet while Baker made his way towards her. She raised one of her hands in a futile attempt to keep him at bay.

'You'd better stay where you are,' she said, staggering backwards. 'I'm betrothed to Iron Eyes. He'd be mighty angry if he knew what you was trying to do.'

The gunman rubbed his hands together and laughed.

'By now Iron Eyes is dead, gal. Can't you hear them Injuns outside the fort? Don't you recall we locked the gates so he couldn't get into the fort?'

Sally could hear the Cheyennes. 'That don't mean he's dead, mister. That just means we got a whole heap of angry Injuns out there in the desert trying to get in.'

A twisted smile creased the gunman's face.

'He's dead,' Baker insisted. 'Them Injuns are ripping him to shreds as we speak. Listen to them.'

The young female felt something stop her retreat. She looked behind her. At the same moment Baker pushed her with both hands.

She fell backwards and landed on the mattress of the cot. As her perfectly formed body bounced he leapt upon her. His hands wandered over her faster than she could stop them. She fought for all she was worth but Baker was far stronger than she was and he had not been controlling a team of six horses since the crack of dawn.

'Get your damn hands off me,' Sally protested as her fists beat against his face.

'Quit tickling me, gal,' Baker mocked.

She wriggled and squirmed but it was useless. Baker was like a bull with a young cow. His hands roamed all over her as he used his weight to pin her down.

Her eyes widened when she felt his hands examining her assets lustfully. He tore her shirt apart and drooled down on her.

'Get the hell off me, you dumb galoot,' she shouted.

'I will when I'm through,' Baker answered. His hands continued to examine every inch of her flesh. She blinked hard and helplessly watched the gunman as he frantically explored her.

'Hold on there a cotton-picking minute,' Sally shouted angrily at Baker. 'That's my chests.'

'Are you enjoying it?' Baker asked. His face moved closer to her ear. 'Are you ready for some pleasuring?'

Sally pulled her arm from under his hefty body and punched Baker across his jaw. His head rocked on his neck as the power of the blow registered.

'How'd you like that pleasuring?' she screamed up at him.

The angry punch had taken Baker by surprise. His left hand clutched at her throat as his right fist shook in violent warning.

'Do that again and I'll knock you senseless, missy,' he hissed angrily. 'Savvy?'

Sally pouted and nodded meekly at the lusty gunman. She fluttered her eyelashes at Baker.

'I'm sorry,' she whimpered. 'I'm so very sorry.'

'That's better. Now just you lie there.' Baker grinned and started to try to unbutton the stud of her pants. He did not expect or see the punch which Sally smashed into the side of his jaw.

The gunman flew off the cot, hit the floor and rolled into the whitewashed wall.

Squirrel Sally got up from the bed. She glared at him and kissed her skinned knuckles. She tried to fasten her shirt but Baker had ripped every one of its buttons off its frayed material. Both her fists were clenched as she secured her pants stud.

'I'm so sorry I ain't got my Winchester, mister,' she said, shaking her fists at the startled Baker. 'I'd have blown your head off your damn shoulders if I had. My chests are for only one man and you ain't him.'

Lane Baker nursed his aching jaw and got back to his feet. He was smiling again as he brushed himself down and moved towards the snarling female.

'If there's one thing I like it's a female with vinegar in her veins,' he said. Quickly he jumped in front of the door and blocked her escape. 'Let's wrestle.'

Sally watched him rub his hands together expectantly, then she squared up to the big gunman. She waved her fists at him.

'You got that dumb look on your face again,' she yelled at Baker as he put himself between the door and herself. 'Stay where you are or I'll be forced to stomp you.'

'I reckon that'll be just fine, gal,' Baker said. 'I

can't think of anyone I'd rather get stomped by.'

Squirrel Sally was confused. 'You sure are anxious to get stomped, mister.'

Sally watched as Baker placed his hands on his leather gunbelt and grinned across the room at her.

'You're the most tempting critter I ever longed for,' he muttered lustfully. 'You sure know how to excite a man and no mistake.'

Baker unbuckled his belt and lowered his guns to the floor. A twisted smile came to his face again as he slowly advanced towards her once more.

'Oh hell!' Sally grumbled. 'Not again.'

THIRTEEN

A chorus of laughter sounded in the bounty hunter's ears as he knelt below the high parapet. Arrows continued to fly from the bows of the whooping Cheyennes as they vainly attempted to slay the creature they blamed for killing the five young bucks.

Yet even though it appeared that Iron Eyes was done for, the severely wounded bounty hunter was unconcerned by the Indians who were pounding on the gates of the fort. All he could think about was the men who surrounded him on the battlements as he knelt among them.

Iron Eyes remained silently watching his blood drip from his savage wounds on to the sunbaked surface of the stones. He had not moved a muscle for more than five minutes as Waldo Schmitt and Fairbanks's men grew bolder and braver.

He refused to acknowledge any of their taunts. Nothing it seemed could rile the infamous figure. He remained like a statue frozen in the position he had adopted moments before.

The gunmen poked his gore-covered carcass with their rifles and six-shooters, but nothing seemed able to penetrate the invisible shield he had surrounded himself with.

To all intents and purposes the bounty hunter might have been as dead as some said he actually was. Yet what none of the six men who encircled him knew was that Iron Eyes was absorbing every insult and mindless physical attack until he was ready to strike.

The injured bounty hunter had needed time to rest.

He required time to muster up enough strength in order to fight.

Every passing heartbeat was giving him that energy.

As he knelt with his head lowered he felt his fiery temper start to ignite deep inside his pitifully thin body. The flames of retribution had burst into an inferno and he was fuelled by them. He snorted through his flared nostrils and eyed his tormentors.

Iron Eyes was like a coiled sidewinder waiting for the opportunity to sink its fangs into its prey. The fire within him grew more intense as he flexed every sinew in readiness.

No stick of dynamite with its fuse lit could have posed a more dangerous threat to the men who continued to kick and hit his motionless body.

Through the long strands of limp hair Iron Eyes could see most of them. His instincts told him exactly where the men unseen behind him were. They betrayed their position by the words they spilled over his back.

Iron Eyes sucked air into his lungs. Faster and faster he breathed in the dry desert air as though he were attempting to inflate his battered and bruised torso.

Directly in front of him Waldo Schmitt stood a few feet from the edge of the high parapet. The wanted outlaw kept poking the hefty barrel of his .45 into Iron Eyes' head but the kneeling man felt no pain.

To the right of Schmitt the rotund Fairchild stood holding a carbine in his hands. To the right of Iron Eyes' shoulder Slim Brewster ranted down at him. Just beyond Brewster Saul Davis hovered like someone who only truly felt brave when he was clutching a rifle.

Tom Carter and Pedro Cortez were standing just behind the bounty hunter. Iron Eyes listened to them as they grew more and more nervous at the sight of the angry Cheyenne braves pounding on the gates below the lofty parapet.

Every fibre of the bounty hunter's tortured form had been tightened in preparation for what he was about to do. His long thins fingers spread out from their knuckles as Iron Eyes tensed himself.

Then to the total surprise of his captors Iron Eyes struck. He charged towards Schmitt. The grim bounty hunter rammed Schmitt in his belly with his bowed head so violently the outlaw went flying backwards off the stone parapet. The outlaw fell and landed heavily on his back in the courtyard.

Before the dust had time to rise around the winded outlaw, Iron Eyes turned and grabbed the barrel of Fairchild's rifle and swung him into Carter. The two men collided. Fairchild stumbled on to his rump while Carter tripped over the wall and fell into the crowd of whooping Cheyennes. The gunman's screams ceased as the Indians engulfed him.

The flashing of their knives and tomahawks

danced along the walls of the fortress.

Totally stunned, Pedro Cortez drew his six-shooter and fired at the fast moving bounty hunter. But Iron Eyes did not notice the lethal lead, which vainly tried to find its target. He kicked out a long leg and buckled Davis. Iron Eyes then leapt on to the bewildered Brewster.

As another fearful shot left the barrel of Cortez's smoking gun, the bounty hunter ensured that it was Brewster who was hit and not himself. His bony grip turned the gunman to face the Mexican as his bullet ripped into him. A choking squeal came from the big man as Iron Eyes released his grip. Brewster fell lifelessly forward and crashed on to his face. Like a desert twister Iron Eyes spun on his heels and jumped on to the stunned Saul Davis. The gunman shook the skeletal figure off his shoulders and then aimed his rifle at Iron Eyes.

The Winchester spat a bullet at the bounty hunter. It came so close that Iron Eyes felt the heat of the lead ball burn his face.

The bounty hunter did not give Davis enough time to cock his rifle again. He lowered his head and charged like a raging bull straight into Davis. The hapless gunman was sent tumbling over the battlements and fell into the courtyard. The sound of his neck snapping filled the air just as Cortez cocked and fired his gun again.

The shot might have hit a fatter man. Like a ravenous cougar, Iron Eyes threw his bloody body across the distance between himself and the Mexican. The bounty hunter caught Cortez around the neck.

Both men crashed heavily into the wall. As Iron Eyes pulled his Bowie knife from the neck of his boot he saw the blood spilling from the head of the unblinking Mexican.

Iron Eyes released his grip and pushed the corpse away from him. The dead Mexican slid over the fortress wall and hung there above the raging Indians.

Suddenly a volley of arrows came up from the Indians' bows below. They struck with terrifying accuracy: none of the arrows missed Cortez.

The blood-covered bounty hunter staggered to his feet and hovered with the long-bladed knife in his hand amid the scene of death and destruction he had created.

His grim glare swept the area in search of the one man he knew had survived his onslaught. It did not take Iron Eyes long to spot what he had been looking for.

His eyes narrowed and fixed upon the crawling Otis Fairchild, who was vainly attempting to escape the fury of the wounded bounty hunter.

'Where do you reckon you're going, fat man?' Iron Eyes grunted. He staggered towards the Indian agent. 'I want me a word with you.'

Fairchild glanced at the hideous creature that was making his way towards him. He stopped crawling when he saw the savage look in the bullet-coloured eyes.

'What kinda critter are you?' Fairchild asked, forcing his shaking body back up and on to his feet.

'Hell, I'm the kind of critter that don't like being pistol-whipped, mister,' Iron Eyes replied. He stepped over the bodies that separated them. 'I owe you a beating and I intend paying up in full.'

As Fairchild spread his arms to either side of him he saw a discarded rifle a few feet from his grasp. His fat hands snatched the Winchester off the ground and cocked its mechanism until it was primed for action. Fairchild grinned as his corrupt mind told him that he had the advantage. He was armed with a rifle and the hideous blood-soaked creature had only a knife.

Iron Eyes stayed his advance.

'I wouldn't try to use that toothpick if I was you,

fat man,' he warned.

Otis Fairchild ignored the warning. He levelled the rifle at the hideous creature who was facing him beside the parapet.

'You can keep your advice for someone who needs it, Iron Eyes,' the Indian agent grunted. He raised the weapon to his shoulder. 'Even you can't bluff a bullet into missing your sorrowful hide.'

Fairchild watched in awe as he saw the bounty hunter, moving faster than he had ever seen anyone move before, throw the Bowie knife at him with every scrap of his dwindling strength behind it.

His eyes widened in horror as the honed blade came straight at him.

The agent tried to move out of the way but it was far too late. The Bowie knife sank into his chest right up to its hilt and knocked Fairchild backwards. The agent felt the rifle fall from his hands before he experienced the strange sensation in his chest.

Fairchild stumbled and dropped to the ground.

He did not see the blood spread out from the knife's hilt, soaking his shirt in crimson gore. His dead eyes did not see anything after the honed blade had skewered a path into his heart.

Iron Eyes leaned over Fairchild and pulled the

Bowie knife out of the agent's chest. He wiped the blade clean with the ragged tails of his long trail coat and walked to the top of the stone steps. The noise of the Indians pounding at the gates grew louder below him. The bounty hunter glanced under the archway as the great wooden portal creaked and strained against the determined Cheyennes as they tried to burst into the fortress.

They were still baying for blood.

His blood.

As long as the gates held firm, Iron Eyes knew he was safe but he realized that once the Cheyennes breached the fort's defences it was only a matter of time before his sorrowful hide joined those of his countless enemies in the bowels of Hell.

Iron Eyes looked down at the sandy ground to where his pair of matched Navy Colts had been discarded by the gunmen. Both weapons jutted out from the blood-coloured sand. Ignoring his fearsome injuries, he walked down the steps towards his prized weaponry. Then he suddenly noticed that the outlaw Schmitt was not where he should be.

Schmitt had landed on his back in the sand, but now only the imprint of the outlaw's body remained. Iron Eyes was troubled to realize that the fall had not killed the valuable man he had chased for weeks.

The bounty hunter paused.

His eyes darted around the courtyard in search of the elusive outlaw. Suddenly a shot resounded around the high-walled courtyard.

Iron Eyes felt the sudden impact. His left shoulder was forcibly punched back. The emaciated hunter fell against the stone wall. Then he felt the warmth of blood trickling down inside his coat sleeve. His eyes saw the scarlet trails of gore run freely over his wrist and hand.

Then another shot took a chunk of stone out of the wall just above his head.

Iron Eyes leapt from the steps and landed in a crouched position just ten feet from one of his trusty weapons. He was about to advance on the guns when another echoing bullet kicked sand up just feet away from his boots.

The bounty hunter pressed his spine against the wall.

His eyes searched for Schmitt in the large courtyard. He could not see the outlaw but he knew where he was hiding. The clouds of gunsmoke hung in the acrid air just behind one of the prairie schooners.

His eyes narrowed and focused between the

wheel spokes. He could see the outlaw crouched beyond the furthest wheel.

'If only I had me my guns,' he snarled. 'I'd put an end to this right now.'

Iron Eyes gripped his trusty knife but knew that even a blade as keen as his could never compete with bullets from a handgun.

'I gotta get to my guns,' he vowed.

Another deafening gunshot erupted from behind the wagon, sending a red-hot taper towards the cornered Iron Eyes. The bullet ricocheted off the stone steps beside him, sending debris showering over his already tormented body. His hands brushed the hot dust off his shoulders as he stared at the two guns again.

Iron Eyes snarled under his breath angrily. 'Let's see how good a shot you really are, Waldo.'

The thin figure dashed across the sand as even more shots blasted at him from across the vast yard. The determined bounty hunter snatched up one of the Navy Colts and then rolled towards its twin.

He cocked the gun's hammer as he came to a halt on his belly beside his other gun. As the outlaw's bullets tore up the sand that surrounded the prostrate bounty hunter, Iron Eyes began to blast his reply with both his Navy Colts.

Shafts of deadly venom criss-crossed the court-yard.

With smoke trailing from his gun barrels Iron Eyes rolled across the sand until his blood-soaked body came to a rest behind a dry trough. Bullets from Schmitt's guns had trailed the bounty hunter's every movement but none had added to the wounded man's already gruesome injuries. Chunks of wood were ripped from the trough as Schmitt vainly tried to be rid of the bounty hunter. Covered in smouldering sawdust, Iron Eyes shook the spent casings from his weapons and hastily reloaded the guns with fresh bullets from his deep trail coat pockets.

'You missed your chance, Schmitt,' Iron Eyes yelled out while his fingers work feverishly to push the bullets into his guns' chambers. 'You should have killed me when you had the chance. Now it's too late. Now I'm gonna kill you.'

'Big talk, bounty hunter,' the outlaw screamed across the courtyard before unleashing another barrage of bullets in the direction of the mocking Iron Eyes' voice.

With his guns reloaded Iron Eyes scurried the length of the trough and peered around its corner. Gunsmoke hung in the late afternoon sunshine.

His eyes narrowed and squinted at the covered wagon.

Schmitt maintained his position just behind the large rear wheels of the flatbed and kept firing at the trough. Iron Eyes could see the outlaw's legs behind the wheel and he raised one of his Navy Colts.

The bounty hunter closed one eye and aimed at the outlaw.

For what seemed a lifetime Iron Eyes watched his target as Schmitt moved close to the saddle horses tethered behind the tailgate of the heavily laden wagon and kept firing his .45.

Iron Eyes squeezed the trigger of one of his guns.

A brilliant plume of yellow lightning flashed from the barrel of the Navy Colt.

He watched as the outlaw fell on to his side clutching his bleeding leg. Iron Eyes stood and marched across the courtyard towards Schmitt with both his guns in his bony hands. His thumbs pulled back on his hammers. The sound of the guns' hammers clicking filled the hot smoke-filled air as the bounty hunter readied his weaponry.

As Iron Eyes rounded the wagon he was greeted by a deafening blast. A bullet cut through the sunlight and passed within inches of its target. Schmitt

142

lay on the ground holding his bleeding thigh with one hand while the other gripped his six-shooter.

Iron Eyes did not wait for the outlaw to cock his gun again. He raised both his Navy Colts and calmly squeezed their triggers. Two deafening bullets hit Schmitt dead centre and knocked him on to his back.

With his smoking guns held firmly at waist height the emotionless Iron Eyes strode to where the outlaw lay in a pool of his own gore. He stared down at Schmitt and spat at the wanted man.

'I told you I was gonna kill you,' Iron Eyes growled. 'I never break me a promise.'

He pushed both his guns into his deep pockets and turned round. One of the gunmen had claimed that Squirrel Sally had been spirited away by one of the agent's other hired gunmen.

Iron Eyes moved like a silent phantom around the wagons and livestock in search of the female. As he rounded the stagecoach and paced beside the team of exhausted horses he heard a faint sound.

He paused beside the lead horse and grabbed its bridle while he tried to work out where the sound had come from. The courtyard was huge and flanked on three sides by various stone structures.

His keen eyesight perceived the tracks left by

Sally's bare feet in the sand. He reached the spot where she had been knocked out and had fallen. Iron Eyes then noticed the imprints of a rider's boots. They were leading to one of the large buildings, and alongside them the sand had been stirred up, as though the wearer of the boots had been dragging a heavy load.

'That critter must have bin dragging little Squirrel,' Iron Eyes hissed through gritted teeth.

A sudden fury overwhelmed the lean bounty hunter. He followed the tracks towards the living quarters. Iron Eyes had always refused to admit that he felt anything for the feisty youngster yet the look on his disfigured face told a different story.

There was a fury raging in the bounty hunter.

It was a fury that would only be appeased when he encountered the gunman who had abducted Squirrel Sally and had taught the man a lesson. Iron Eyes was about to enter through the open doorway when the sound of the fortress gates being pounded drew his attention. His narrowed eyes could see the gates moving under the constant pressure of the Cheyennes.

Time was running out.

He knew that it was only a matter of minutes before the Cheyennes broke through the fort's defences and came seeking revenge for the young braves.

Iron Eyes shook his head. He knew that it was impossible for him even to try and tell them that he was not responsible for their deaths. Then he heard raised voices come from deep inside the building's corridors.

One of those raised voices belonged to Squirrel Sally, he told himself. She could deafen a mountain lion with her roar.

He continued into the living quarters.

The noisy ruckus was coming from his left. The gaunt bounty hunter lowered his head and marched towards the noise. With every stride of his long thin legs the sound grew louder.

Iron Eyes turned a corner and paused. In front of him along the corridor were more than six closed doors. He could hear the sounds of an excited man and a furious female coming from one of the rooms but he was not sure which one. He could also hear furniture being broken.

Iron Eyes set off along the passageway, pausing to listen at each door. As he reached the third room the sound of shattering glass or china filled his ears. His female companion was holding her own by the sound of it, he thought.

Iron Eyes inhaled deeply and held on to the brass doorknob. He was about to turn it when suddenly the entire door gave way and Lane Baker came flying through. Iron Eyes was hit not only by the wooden door panels but by Baker as well.

The bounty hunter was flung against the opposite wall as wood and the overweight gunman crashed into his frail frame. A shot came blistering from the room and ricocheted off the wall above both men's heads.

'That's my gun, missy,' Baker ranted as she emerged from the bedroom. 'I want it back.'

'I'm keeping this hogleg,' Sally snarled, firing another shot over the man's head. 'You can have the bullets though.'

Baker scrambled fearfully to his feet and bolted towards the courtyard. Sally watched his departure, holding the gunman's smoking six-shooter in her hand.

She was about to fire another shot after the fleeing Baker when she saw Iron Eyes beneath the remnants of the busted door.

'Beloved!' she exclaimed.

Iron Eyes looked up at the half-naked female and raised an eyebrow thoughtfully.

'Your chests are hanging out, Squirrel,' he noted

drily. His hands angrily pushed the wood off his bruised and bleeding body.

The petite female helped Iron Eyes to his feet and started to brush him down. The dazed bounty hunter was about to push her away but then was afraid of what he might accidently touch if he tried to do so.

'You come looking for me, Iron Eyes,' she gushed and wrapped herself around him. 'That's so romantic. You come looking for your sweetheart out here in this terrible desert. You must really love me, darling.'

He peeled her off him and shook his head. 'I didn't even know you was here, Squirrel.'

She fluttered her lashes. 'You must have known.'

Iron Eyes started marching after Baker.

'I only came here 'cos a heap of Cheyennes were chasing me, Squirrel,' he said with a sigh. She kept pace with him as they headed towards the sunlight. 'I told you to wait in Dry Wells.'

'It's a good thing I didn't,' Sally retorted. She smiled.

'Why would that be?' He stopped by the door that led to the courtyard and looked down on to the beautiful youngster.

'I found out that them men out there are going

147

to trade guns and whiskey to them Injuns, dearest,' she informed him and pointed at the trio of prairie schooners next to her stagecoach. 'Them wagons are full of rotgut and rifles.'

A crooked grin appeared on his face. 'You say them wagons are full of whiskey and guns, huh?'

She nodded firmly. 'Yep. They sure are.'

Before the bounty hunter could respond a shot came from the courtyard and narrowly missed them both. Iron Eyes went to haul his Navy Colts from his deep coat pockets but before his fingers could reach them he saw Sally raise the gun she was carrying and squeeze its trigger.

With an ear-splitting crack the bullet streaked across the courtyard. It found its target with lethal accuracy. A pitiful cry came from Lane Baker as Sally's shot hit him between the eyes and knocked him off his feet. She and the bounty hunter watched as a rifle fell from his hands.

'Where'd he get the rifle?' Sally wondered.

'There's plenty of rifles and guns scattered around here, Squirrel,' Iron Eyes said, shrugging. 'I killed all the varmints that was toting them.'

'I killed that critter.' Sally nodded firmly, pointing at the body of Baker as blood pumped from his shattered skull.

Iron Eyes patted her on the top of her blond curly mop and cleared his throat.

'Good shot, Squirrel,' he muttered. 'Best head shot I've seen in a coon's age.'

Sally frowned and shook her head. 'I weren't aiming at his head, Iron Eyes. I was aiming at the thing he was using to think with.'

Iron Eyes led his companion out into the blistering sunshine towards the canvas-covered wagons. As they passed the dead Baker, Sally tossed his gun aside and plucked the Winchester up off the sand. She brushed the sand from the rifle and looked up at her gaunt friend.

'That scum-sucker used my own rifle to try and kill us with, Iron Eyes,' she said as they reached the tailgate of the first wagon. 'This is my rifle.'

Iron Eyes pulled the knife from the neck of his boot, slid its honed blade through the canvas and lifted it. He stared into the back of the wagon at box after box of rifles and ammunition.

'There's enough rifles and bullets here to start a war, Squirrel,' he gasped in horror. 'By my reckoning that agent critter intended trading this arsenal for something they've got.'

'What would Injuns have that's worth all them guns?' Sally wondered.

'Damned if I know,' he replied. He set off towards the next wagon.

She followed the tall figure to the wagon and watched as he repeated his action with his Bowie knife. Iron Eyes lifted the canvas and peered over the tailgate.

'What's in this 'un?' she asked.

'Whiskey. Bottles and barrels of whiskey,' Iron Eyes replied. He walked to the last of the agent's wagons. Again he cut the canvas and looked inside.

'What they got in this 'un?' Sally asked.

'Nothing. There ain't nothing at all in this one,' Iron Eyes answered and turned to face her. 'They must have intended using this one to carry something out of here, Squirrel.'

The sound of the fort gates creaking under the constant battering of the Cheyennes drew their attention. Sally gripped his coat sleeve fearfully.

'What's m-making that ruckus, Iron Eyes?' she stammered.

'Injuns, Squirrel,' he replied. 'Mighty ornery Injuns.'

'What do they want?'

'Me.'

FINALE

Iron Eyes had a plan. It was risky but it was the only plan he could think of as the wooden gates started to give way under the constant onslaught of the Cheyennes. What time he had left before they eventually broke through the fort's defences was running out fast. He grabbed Sally's tiny shoulders.

'Listen up, Squirrel. You gotta do exactly as I tell you. We ain't got much time left.'

Sally nodded and listened.

'You water your stagecoach team and then climb up on to the driver's board,' Iron Eyes said. 'Then you slide down into the box and hide there.'

'But Iron Eyes . . .' her youthful voice had never sounded so frightened before, 'what about you?'

'Don't fret about me, Squirrel.' His bony fingers

touched her cheek gently. 'Do as I tell you. I have things to do but when I'm through I'll be climbing up there with you.'

The beautiful female nodded her head and started to fill buckets with the precious water from the well just as she had been instructed. Whatever her beloved Iron Eyes had planned she knew it had to be done quickly.

The bounty hunter released the dead men's horses from the rear of the wagons. He pulled a cutting rope from one of the saddle horns and looped it over his shoulder. He then waved his arms and frightened the saddle mounts away from the wagons.

He swung on his heels to face the vehicles. Iron Eyes pulled the pins on the tailgates of both of the loaded wagons, and then dragged a box full of whiskey bottles from the flatbed of one of the wagons and carried it to the other wagon that was filled with scores of rifles and boxes of ammunition.

The bounty hunter used the grip of one of his guns to break the box open. His teeth pulled the corks from the necks of several bottles, then he poured the contents liberally over the rifles and the bed of the wagon. Within minutes he had emptied the liquor out of a dozen bottles.

He glanced at the fort gates and then at Sally as she finished watering all six of her horses just as he had told her to. As she climbed up the side of the stagecoach Iron Eyes ran back to the wagon filled with boxes of whiskey and started to smash the boxes open. The interior of the wagon stank with the sour aroma of cheap rotgut whiskey. He lifted one of the opened boxes off the flatbed and ran back to the ammunition wagon.

This time he placed the box under the wagon and used his Navy Colt to shatter the glass bottles. The crude whiskey fumes filled his flared nostrils.

Iron Eyes was not finished yet.

He grabbed hold of the lifeless Waldo Schmitt, hauled him off the ground and up on to his shoulder. Fighting his own fatigue and brutal injuries he ignored the pain that ripped through him and carried the body to the rear of the stagecoach.

Iron Eyes dropped Schmitt on to the stagecoach trunk, pulled its canvas cover down and buckled its straps.

'Shame I ain't got the time to hunt down Miller,' he muttered as he considered the reward money he would collect if he lived long enough to get out of the fort.

The bounty hunter was about to run along the

side of the vehicle when the courtyard resounded to the noise of the large gates breaking away from their hinges. A cloud of dust rose around the huge gates as they crashed to the ground. The dust was thick enough to mask at least some of his activities, he thought.

Iron Eyes was trapped at the rear of the stage. His narrowed eyes watched as the Cheyenne warriors came cautiously into the fortress with their bows and knives in readiness.

His mind raced.

The only thing he knew for certain was that he dare not allow them to get their hands on the arsenal Fairchild and his cronies had brought to the fort.

The bounty hunter exhaled and then dug his last cigar from his trail coat pocket. He watched the Cheyennes as they were drawn closer and closer to the wagons by the aroma of the whiskey fumes.

Iron Eyes climbed up on the stagecoach's large rear wheel and balanced there as he ignited a match with his thumbnail. He shielded the flame from being seen through the coach windows and puffed on the cigar until its tip was glowing red.

The thin figure climbed along the side of the stagecoach and then carefully hauled his lean frame up on to its roof. He placed the cutting rope on the driver's seat before turning to face the whiskey-doused prairie schooners. He lay there with the cigar between his lips.

Most of the Cheyennes had reached the wagons and were cautiously investigating their contents. Iron Eyes slid along the roof and looked towards the gates. They lay shattered on the ground.

Iron Eyes sucked in as much smoke as he could, then removed the cigar from his lips. He carefully held the tobacco stick between his fingers, then flicked it over the heads of the curious warriors.

The glowing cigar hit the liquor-soaked canvas and dropped down into the pool of spilled whiskey beneath the prairie schooner laden with boxes of rifles and ammunition.

The whiskey fumes erupted into flame. Within seconds the fire had crept up the side of the tailgate and had engulfed the wagon.

The startled Cheyennes were forced back by the heat and flames. They could not understand what was happening and they vainly tried to see what was inside the burning wagon. The burning canvas floated on the waves of heat and set the other wagon ablaze.

Using the total confusion to his advantage, Iron

Eyes slid across the coach roof and then dropped unseen down into the driver's box beside the confused Sally.

His hushed her little cry of surprise by pressing a bony hand across her lips.

The bounty hunter reached up and released the vehicle's brake pole. He then stood up long enough to whip the reins across the backs of the six-horse team, then dropped from view again. The startled team bolted towards the shattered gates with the long vehicle in tow. Iron Eyes steered the team through the gateway and out into the desert.

As the stagecoach charged through the abandoned painted ponies he stood up and cracked the reins again. The stagecoach thundered away from the fortress across the crimson ground as Iron Eyes climbed on to the driver's seat.

'What did you do?' Sally asked, clambering out of the box and to sit beside the bounty hunter.

Iron Eyes glanced over his shoulder.

'Any minute now you'll find out, Squirrel,' he replied in a low drawl.

Her face looked confused. 'What in tarnation are you talking about, darling?'

Suddenly the roaring flames in the fort turned into a series of mighty explosions which erupted from the centre of the stone edifice. As debris and black smoke rose into the darkening sky more spine-chilling blasts could be heard and seen as the boxes of ammunition discharged their fury.

The entire desert shuddered beneath the wheels of the fleeing stage. Sally gripped Iron Eyes' arm as her unblinking eyes stared at the fearsome flames and blasts that repeatedly shook the entire desert.

'What the hell did you do?' Sally stammered as, wide-eyed, she watched the massive explosions which rattled the very fabric of the fortress. 'How did you make everything blow up like that?'

With choking dust tormenting his already brutal-ized lungs the bounty hunter expertly steered the stagecoach further and further away from the mayhem he had created. Iron Eyes gritted his teeth as debris landed all around the speeding vehicle. Sally shook his sleeve.

'Answer me, Iron Eyes,' she insisted. 'How'd you blow up that fort back there?'

The setting sun cast its eerie light across the pair perched high on driver's seat of the stagecoach. Iron Eyes glanced at the half-naked Sally as her tiny hands gripped the long seat beneath her rump. The sight of her white knuckles amused the skeletal driver. He relented.

'Well, the truth is I kinda poured a whole heap of that rotgut liquor over them wagons' cargo. Then I tossed my cigar into the whiskey-soaked mess,' he grunted with a smug twinkle in his eyes. 'Reckon the whiskey caught alight, Squirrel. It sure took them Cheyennes by surprise when them bullets exploded.'

Kneeling on the well-sprung seat, Sally gripped the baggage rail. She looked over the roof of the rocking stagecoach as flames from another massive explosion licked the sky. She spun around and nodded.

'Yep, bullets and whiskey do get kinda ornery when you set fire to them, Iron Eyes,' she commented as the stagecoach continued on into the desolate terrain.

'They sure do, Squirrel,' her companion agreed.

Sally picked up the coiled cutting rope set between them and stared at it with some curiosity. She waved it under his nose as the bounty hunter held on to the long leathers.

'What the hell did you bring this rope for?' she innocently asked. 'You figuring on hanging someone?'

Iron Eyes pointed ahead at his magnificent palomino stallion which was standing stubbornly in its ornate Mexican livery a few hundred yards ahead of them. The animal spotted the stagecoach heading towards it and then took flight. The last rays of the dying sun danced across the cream-coloured horse as it fled from its gruesome master.

'Why'd I bring a rope? How else am I gonna catch that nag, Squirrel?' Iron Eyes asked as he urged the six-horse team to continue in pursuit of his prized mount.

Sally wriggled her toes and leaned close to him.

'This was a real waste of your time and blood when you think about it,' she commented. 'You didn't capture them outlaws you was chasing and you got hurt.'

'I sure did catch me one of them *hombres*, Squirrel,' he differed. 'I got me the dead carcass of Waldo Schmitt back in your trunk. I didn't have time to find his pard. When we find a town I'm gonna collect that reward money.'

Sally looked down at her bare chest and searched all around her firm torso in the vain hope of finding her weathered trail gear.

'Have you got any notion what happened to my shirt?' she asked as the long vehicle thundered after the handsome stallion.

Iron Eyes shrugged.

'Damned if I know what happened to it.' He winced as he felt the savage raw gash in his side rub against his own shirt. 'Are you any good with a darning needle, Squirrel?'

'Hell, I ain't gonna make me no new shirt, Iron Eyes,' she purred, nestling into him. 'You can buy me one with the bounty money.'

Iron Eyes rolled his eyes and then covered her soft flesh with the protection of his trail coat. His piercing eyes stared at the palomino stallion ahead of them. He was about to speak when he felt her small hands and even smaller fingers mischievously teasing his bloodstained pants leg.

'You'll stay buck naked unless you don't quit groping me, Squirrel,' Iron Eyes said as an inscrutable smile teased his scarred features. 'Not that you'd give a damn.'